VIENNA MASQUERADE

On the death of her beloved Austrian grandmother, Kristal Hastings decides to go to Austria to search for relatives she has never met. When she meets Rodolfo von Steinberg, the young cousin of Baron Gustav von Steinberg, who had been her grandmother's lover many years ago, an instant attraction flares between them. But how can she give her love to Rudi when he is already promised to another . . . ?

Books by Lorna McKenzie
in the Linford Romance Library:

PICTURES IN PROVENCE
TWENTIETH-CENTURY PIRATE
TO SARA — WITH LOVE
STORM DAMAGE
JILTED

LORNA McKENZIE

VIENNA MASQUERADE

Complete and Unabridged

LINFORD
Leicester

First published in Great Britain in 1994

Originally published under the title
'Secret Love' by Nora Fountain

First Linford Edition
published 1997

British Library CIP Data

McKenzie, Lorna
    Vienna masquerade.—Large print ed.—
Linford romance library
1. English fiction—20th century
2. Large type books
I. Title
823.9′14 [F]

ISBN 0–7089–5038–8

Published by
F. A. Thorpe (Publishing) Ltd.
Anstey, Leicestershire

Set by Words & Graphics Ltd.
Anstey, Leicestershire
Printed and bound in Great Britain by
T. J. International Ltd., Padstow, Cornwall

This book is printed on acid-free paper

1

A SMILE tugged at Kristal Hastings' mouth as she approached the cheerful, blond giant wielding the name-board with her name on it. She had never been met this way before.

"Guten tag!" she greeted him, adding in German, "I'm Kristal Hastings. I wasn't expecting a welcoming committee!"

"You're not getting one — just me." He grinned back.

His eyes did a rapid inventory of her five feet ten inches of slender, curvy womanhood.

She knew she looked good. For comfort she had slung a cinnamon jacket over a cream, silk shirt and matching linen trousers. A cinnamon, pull-on hat sat atop her neatly-styled, blonde hair. Gold earrings dangled from her shell-like earlobes, matching her bracelet and the elegant, Swiss watch at her wrist. At twenty-four she looked exactly what she was — the PR representative of an exclusive fashion-house. A very classy lady.

"Are you Rodolfo von Steinberg?" she enquired hopefully.

That was the man she had written to. The reply had not been over-friendly, yet this blond giant was remarkably so. He threw back his head and laughed.

"I'm afraid not," he replied. "I'm Johann Schmit — general dogsbody and chauffeur. Let's go."

She'd had no idea what kind of welcome to expect, nor indeed who made up the household of the von Steinbergs. She just knew that, with Analiese, her beloved, Austrian grand-mother and only living relative, now dead, she had nothing to lose in coming here, in search of Austrian relatives.

She had intended to hire a taxi. She would have no difficulty in giving directions, for she and her

2

grandmother had frequently conversed in German from her earliest days. Today she had listened enthralled to the lilting, Viennese accents all around, as she claimed her two cases from the revolving carousel. Hoisting them on to a trolley she had topped them with the tote-bag she had kept with her on the plane and, after the usual formalities, had set off with some trepidation towards the exit.

Other passengers straggled in groups or alone as they neared the reception area. People waved and smiled in greeting, calling out to friends and relatives as they arrived. If only there was someone for her, she had thought, fighting down a rare attack of self-pity at her lone status.

Then she had come to the name-boards, and done a double-take on seeing her own name — Kristal Hastings. Someone was waiting for her.

Johann was certainly friendly enough, but she still faced the hurdle of meeting

3

Herr von Steinberg, whose reply to her first letter had been so dismissive. In her second letter, she had informed him that she fully intended to visit Vienna, but would stay in a hotel, and contact him from there. This had brought a grudging invitation to his home.

Dispensing with her trolley, Johann fixed her tote-bag under one arm, picked up a suitcase in each hand, and strode off towards the exit. Kristal almost had to run to keep up with him.

Outside, the mid-afternoon sky was the clearest blue she had ever seen and, after leaving behind a typical English April day of sunshine and showers, mostly the latter, she felt her spirits lift. There was no time to stop and stare, though. Johann was already plunging across the Tarmac towards a long, sleek, black Mercedes with tinted windows. He quickly stowed the luggage in the boot before opening the back door and gesturing for her to climb in.

As she did so she gave him a beautiful smile, happy to be in Vienna at last, revealing perfect white teeth and lighting her blue eyes to sapphires.

"Thank you, Johann," she said, slightly breathless from their hasty exit.

The door shut with a satisfying clunk.

"Good-afternoon," came a deep, melodic voice in barely-accented English.

She swung round. At the other end of the seat, half-turned towards her, sat a large, dark-haired, broad-shouldered man. His light-hazel eyes glowed amber under heavy, black brows. Her smile faded as she took in the harsh, granite features and hostile expression. Though probably no more than thirty-five, there was a wealth of experience and knowledge in those penetrating eyes. He moved restively and her eyes were drawn to a flat stomach and long, muscled thighs under a dark, superbly-tailored suit. His tie was awry, his top shirt button undone, as if he had recently left the office and was officially off-duty.

He was, Kristal had to acknowledge, the most devastatingly handsome man she had ever encountered, but, if his intention was to intimidate her, for whatever reason, then he was going to be disappointed.

"Hello, and who are you?" she enquired.

"I am Rodolfo Wolfgang Gustav von Steinberg."

Kristal felt her stomach muscles contract as she tried to control the urge to giggle. Pompous swine! The giggle was gaining ground, but she managed to transform it into one of her loveliest smiles.

"How do you do? I'm delighted to meet you," she assured him sincerely. "What do your friends call you?"

Was that a glint of humour in those deep-set, black-lashed eyes?

"My friends call me Rodolfo. The family — Rudi."

"So — do I call you Rudi?"

"Certainly not! We haven't established what you are to our family, if anything, but I shall make it my business to find out just what you're after."

"Wh-what do you mean?" she asked uncertainly, thoroughly shaken by his harsh words.

"I mean, do you make a habit of scanning the Times' obituary column in the hope of unearthing some rich, deceased relative?"

The unspoken accusation shocked Kristal to the core. She recalled the morning when she had scanned the obituary column of the Times, to check the entry relating to her grandmother: *Hastings, Analiese, dearly-loved grandmother of Kristal. . .* There had not been many entries that day and her eyes had run idly down the rest of the column, arrested by the final entry: *von Steinberg, Baron Gustav, brother of Mathilde, beloved Opa of Gabriele and cousin of Rodolfo . . .* She was beginning to understand the reason for

Rodolfo's apparent hostility! She forced herself to respond calmly.

"Only when I'm looking for the entry regarding my grandmother — my last, known relative."

She caught a glimpse of uncertainty and something softer in his eyes. Pity? She certainly didn't want pity from this man. She wasn't sure what she did want, but not that. He leaned towards her and her short, straight nose, with its hint of a bump at the bridge, caught the scent of his musky aftershave. Her soft lips quivered and she felt a sudden flush reddening her cheeks. What on earth was happening to her? She glanced away to try to compose herself. A long finger touched her pointed chin and turned her face back to his.

"Is that the truth? Did your grandmother die recently?" he demanded harshly.

"Yes," she replied brusquely.

His hand fell away and she missed his touch. Yet she could still feel it.

Her skin felt seared by it.

"And your parents?" he enquired more gently.

"Their yacht overturned ten years ago when I was fourteen. I was staying with my grandmother at the time — I never left."

They lapsed into silence. He produced a lap-top computer and proceeded to work on it. Surreptitiously, she watched his lean fingers tapping away on the machine, fingers she was sure would know how to caress a woman —

Horrified by the direction of her thoughts, she forced her attention back to the view through the tinted window.

They crossed the Danube and headed for the outskirts of town. Eventually, Johann swung the car beneath a wrought-iron archway linking black-painted, gold-tipped railings, and into the cobbled forecourt of a large, stone-built house. An impressive, porticoed entrance was flanked by long windows on the ground floor. There were three more floors above, including the neat attic windows. "Bring the luggage in, Johann. Josef will take it up."

"Jawohl, mein Herr," Johann replied with a grin.

"You'll stay with me, where I can keep an eye on you."

The front door led into a vestibule, while an inner door revealed a long, wide corridor that cut through the house. There was evidence of wealth on every side. No doubt they did need to be careful, but there was no need to be so abominably rude.

A young maid, dressed neatly in a navy dress with a lace collar, walked briskly towards them.

"Ah, Trudi! Is Fraulein Gabriele at home?"

"Er, no, sir. She went shopping."

"That was this morning."

"Yes, sir."

He sighed. "All right. Take my guest's coat and hat and bring some tea to my study. Oh, and tell Gabi I want to see her as soon as she returns."

The study was a very masculine room — buttoned leather, polished mahogany, books and files, and office equipment that included a computer, its colour monitor flickering away. What with that and his portable model, he was obviously a fan of modern technology.

"Now then, tell me why you've come," Rodolfo demanded, once they were seated.

"I thought I explained in my letter."

"You seem to think you're related to the von Steinbergs. Naturally, I want to know what makes you think so. Oh, bring it over here by the fire," he ordered Trudi, as she wheeled in a trolley. "Thanks, we'll manage now."

There was tea in a silver pot and a choice of milk and sugar or lemon slices. There was also a tiered cake-stand with a mouth-watering selection of cakes and pastries.

"Shall I pour?" Kristal offered.

"If you would, please. I take lemon."

11

So did Kristal, so tea was dealt with quickly.

"Do have something to eat, or my cook will be deeply offended."

"I really couldn't — "

"Try one of these," he suggested, selecting a flaky concoction that tasted of lemon and almonds.

"Mmm, delicious," she enthused. "I'd weigh a ton if I ate these every day."

"That I doubt," he said as his eyes ran down the length of her svelte curves and once again she felt her cheeks reddening. Now that they were out of the shade of the car, the effect was all too obvious, and his eyes alighted on her flushed features. She felt like an adolescent, hating him for the effect he was having on her.

"So, what do you want to know?" she snapped.

She noted the amusement in his eyes and hated him all the more for being so aware of what was happening to her.

"You saw Gustav's obituary — on the

12

very same day as your grandmother's?"

"Precisely! It seems they couldn't be together in life, but they were destined to enter the pearly gates together."

"What do you imagine your grandmother was to Gustav?"

"I don't have to imagine — I know! She never made any secret of the fact they were lovers. She met him while she was helping his father with the cataloguing of his vast library. My grandmother was rather well educated for a girl in those days, and probably a great help to the old baron."

"That may be so." He shrugged dismissively. "The library has always been in good order, ever since I can remember. So, what are you telling me? That she seduced the son of the house, Gustav, in fact?"

"No, I'm not!" she retorted angrily. "They fell in love. He asked her to be his wife, and, on the strength of that, they became lovers."

"Go on," he said coldly, disbelief all over his face.

"She became pregnant. Every morning she was horribly sick. One of the staff discovered her secret, and reported it to the housekeeper who, in turn, reported it to a member of the family. As a result, she was dismissed immediately. She begged to be allowed to speak to Gustav, but he had gone on a business trip to Paris that very day. She was told that he had been informed of her story, but that he denied it, and had no wish to see her. She never saw him again."

"He sent her money?"

"Not a penny! He had already denied paternity, don't forget. Not that she would have accepted anything after the way she was treated, though."

"Of course not," he agreed drily. "I can understand Gustav letting her go, once the relationship, if it existed, had run its course. But you're asking me to believe that Gustav allowed a pregnant girl to be thrown out without a penny — or even a reference?"

"Not even that."

"So what did she do?"

"She made for London. It was the late Thirties. War was imminent and the Continent was becoming an increasingly uncomfortable place to be. She found work in a London hotel, where she met David Hastings, an airforce officer, who fell in love with her. He knew that she was pregnant and in love with another man, but he wanted to marry her, anyway. Being a survivor, Analiese, my grandmother, decided that holding a British passport was preferable to being incarcerated for the duration of the war as an undesirable alien.

"Immediately after the wedding ceremony there was an alert, and David Hastings, her brand-new husband, was called away. When his squadron returned, his plane was not among them. David was one of the first casualties of the war and, as a result, the marriage was never consummated. Analiese moved to the country, taking a cottage near David's parents in Dorset.

She had other marriage proposals, despite the shortage of young men on account of the war, but she never married again. She believed she was a jinx for other men, while her heart still belonged to Gustav."

"And David's parents believed the child was their son?"

"Yes. Oh, she wasn't particularly happy about the deception, but it offered a two-way benefit. The baby, my father, Andrew, had grandparents, and, since David had been their only child, they had a baby to love, to make the bitterness of their loss easier to bear."

"Very convenient! Presumably they also helped financially?"

"What if they did? When the war ended, and Andrew went to school, Analiese returned to London, where there was plenty of work, putting libraries to rights after the devastation of the blitz. From that moment on, she was well able to support her son on what she earned. All the money

16

from David's parents was put in trust for Andrew."

"What became of Andrew, your father?"

"He proved quite a scholar. He won a place at Oxford, where he took a first in maths. At his last May Ball there, he met my mother. When he left Oxford, he invested in his own engineering business, later turning to computers. He married my mother as soon as she had finished her degree. He wouldn't allow her to go out to work, though she did write a few children's books — secretly, at first. After his own childhood, he decided a woman's place was in the home."

"He regretted losing his father to the war?"

"Haven't you listened to a word I've been saying? David Hastings was not his father. Analiese never spared him the truth about his own father. As a result, he had incredibly strict morals — I doubt very much that he and my mother anticipated their marriage.

17

My own teens certainly weren't much fun. When I was home from boarding-school, I had to account for every minute I was out of the house. I would never have had a career at all if Mother hadn't been on my side."

"What exactly do you do?"

"I work in PR for Robards' Fashions."

His eyes skimmed the graceful length of her body.

"Why not as a model?"

"They suggested it, actually, when I turned up for my interview, but, although my father was no longer around, I knew he would have disapproved. It's not something I fancied for myself, either. I always wear the firm's clothes, though, as a sort of walking advertisement."

"And have you also inherited your mother's gift for story-telling?"

"As a matter of fact, I have tried my hand at a few children's stories, but so far, I haven't approached a publisher."

"You should, Miss Hastings. I feel

sure you have the gift. I'm sorry you've had a wasted journey."

"What do you mean?"

"Frankly, I don't believe a word about this liaison between your grandmother and old Gustav. I understand how lonely you must feel with not a relative in the world, so, because of that, together with your gift for fantasy, you've come up with a credible story — but not one I'm inclined to believe."

"How dare you!" she burst out, furious at his cold contempt. "You let me pour out the long-hidden secrets of my family, and then call me a liar!"

"I prefer story-teller. Most entertaining! More tea?"

Kristal saw red. She leaped to her feet.

"How dare you sit there and accuse me of lying? You smug, arrogant — "

"Sit down!" he ordered harshly. "Think yourself lucky I'm not having you thrown out right away."

"You don't imagine I'm staying an instant longer in your house, do you?

If you're the last of von Steinbergs, then the sooner the name dies out the better!"

"I said, sit down," he repeated, rising to his feet, all the more threatening for the calm silkiness of his tone.

Thoroughly rattled by now, Kristal made for the door, only to be seized by the arm and swung round to face Rodolfo. His long fingers closed round her shoulders as he towered over her.

"Let me go, you great bully," she demanded, her blue eyes flashing defiance.

His eyes narrowed on her face as if something about her puzzled him. Kristal felt the fight in her evaporate as she became aware of other sensations. His hands burned her skin through the thin, cream silk of her blouse. Deep within her, desire sparked to life and slowly unfurled.

"No," she murmured, denying what was happening as much to herself as to him.

His shrewd, amber eyes gleamed

darkly. Her blue gaze dropped to his mouth and lingered there, fascinated by the sensual arch of his lips. Her legs turned to jelly. Her will-power deserted her as he pulled her slowly towards him till their bodies touched.

She had to pull away, she knew that, but her body refused to obey her mind.

She could feel his hard, muscled chest, pressing against her with a fiery heat. The rest of her body moulded itself to his. He threaded a hand through the gold silk of her hair. She heard his breath catch, and then his lips were on hers.

There was nothing gentle in his kiss. It was a kiss of plunder and demand, and, to her shame afterwards, Kristal answered that demand. Their lips met in the urgency and ferocity of desire. In no way did it resemble the chaste, good-night kisses which she allowed her occasional escort.

She twined her arms round his neck, pulling his head down to prolong the kiss. When he pushed her from him, none too gently, she felt dazed and disorientated. His hands dropped from her shoulders.

"Well, you really are something, Kristal Hastings! Now there's no chance of an inheritance, you make a play for the heir!"

"Why you despicable — " Her hand swung towards his lean, sardonic cheek, but he was too quick for her, and she found her wrist seized once again by those long, mobile fingers, but this time he flung her arm away as if the mere touch disgusted him and returned to his seat.

She stood there for a moment, unsure of her next move but, her legs suddenly so weak they threatened to give way, she, too, sat down. She might be wrong, but she could swear that his heart had been beating as fast as her own, so why was he now acting as if she had been the one to make the first move and instigate that kiss?

Unable to sit still, while her mind

teemed with such thoughts, she reached forward, filled the tea-pot from the hot-water jug and poured herself some more tea. He pushed his cup towards her and she filled it, too.

"Thank you," he muttered as she handed it to him. "So — "

The door swung open and a girl as tall as Kristal herself hurtled into the room.

"Rudi, darling! I've had a wonderful shopping trip. I've bought the most fabulous — " She paused, catching sight of Kristal, and the two girls took stock of each other.

The newcomer was as dark as Kristal was fair. Her glossy, black hair framed a heart-shaped face with a straight nose, softly-rounded cheekbones and eyes like periwinkles. She was tall and slim, her model-girl figure ultra-slender in black trousers and a matching cashmere sweater. Her wide mouth was smiling infectiously and Kristal returned her smile. The other laughed delightedly, a lovely tinkling sound.

"You look like my negative!" she declared.

"Gabi, what on earth are you talking about?" Rodolfo asked with barely-leashed impatience.

Kristal was equally puzzled, wondering if the other girl was slightly crazy.

"Gabi, this is Kristal Hastings, from England."

"Kristal — what a lovely name! Look, Kristal." She urged Kristal to her feet and led her to the gilt-framed mirror opposite the window. "Same height, same figure, same bone-structure — even our eyes are identical. But you're fair, in pale clothes, and I'm dark, in black — like you're my negative, or I'm yours!"

Kristal studied their reflections. The girl was absolutely right. There was an uncanny resemblance between them.

"Our noses are different," she pointed out.

Though equally pretty, her own had that slight bump at the bridge, that lent a certain aristocracy to her face. She

24

met Rodolfo's eyes through the mirror, a glint of satisfaction in her own. He was clearly disconcerted.

"Kristal had some idea she might be a distant cousin of ours."

"He didn't tell you I was coming?" Kristal asked.

Both girls turned accusing eyes on Rodolfo.

"I told no-one. Your letter was only one among many from would-be relations. Gabi, incidentally, is my third cousin, once removed, or some such," he explained, "and Gustav's granddaughter."

"Hello, Gabi." It was too late for formal greetings with this girl, who occupied the position that, but for cruel fate, Kristal herself might have held. "I clearly made a mistake. If you could call me a taxi, Rodolfo."

Gabi laughed her delightful laugh once again.

"Call him Rudi — Rodolfo is so stuffy! And you can't go, Kristal. We must be related. Don't you agree, darling? Tell her she must stay — as long as she likes."

"I see little point," Kristal said quietly, to absolve Rodolfo from ousting her in front of his delightful, young cousin.

"Please, Kristal. You'd be like the sister I never had." She turned to her relative pleadingly. "Rudi?"

"Naturally, you can stay — as Gabi's guest," he grudgingly agreed.

"Wonderful, you'll liven the place up no end. It gets a bit tedious with mostly just old Mathilde and me about the place. Have you seen my grandfather yet?"

2

KRISTAL recoiled in shock. She imagined the funeral would have taken place days ago. In any case, she had an absolute dread of seeing a corpse. She had been considered too young at fourteen to identify her parents' bodies, and she had arrived back from a business trip to Milan too late to be there at the end for her grandmother, dear Analiese.

"We haven't established that I really am family," she said quietly, turning pale. "I hardly think — "

"Opa won't be concerned about that," Gabi replied gaily, using the familiar term for her grandfather. "He'll be only too delighted to see another young face around — "

"What did you say?" Kristal asked faintly, suddenly white as a sheet.

27

"Sit down!" came the stern command from Rudi.

The next instant her head was being forced between her knees. As reality flooded back, she was aware of something approaching an argument between Rudi and Gabi.

"But why didn't you tell her it was joke?"

"Perhaps because you are unique in sharing Gustav's sense of humour!"

"You should have told her straight away, if that's the reason she came!"

"I wanted to find out more about her first. I don't discuss family business with complete strangers."

"Don't be so solemn, darling."

Kristal sat up in time to see Gabi reach up and plant a kiss firmly on those lips that a short time ago had set her own on fire. She felt a stab of envy at the easy familiarity between them, the obvious right of Gabi to kiss Rudi as and when she liked. It reinforced her sense of loneliness. To her surprise, Rudi came and kneeled beside her.

"Are you all right, Kristal?"

He spoke her name gently, pronouncing it as if he had just discovered, and rather liked it.

"Y-yes — it was a shock, that's all."

"I'm sorry. Of course, I intended to tell you. I wish I'd done so sooner — I didn't know Gabi was going to issue her invitation to meet Gustav like that."

"No, of course you didn't," she conceded, "but you could have let me know I was under a misapprehension from the start."

"I have apologised," he reminded her.

"You will want to meet him," Gabi put in, "now that you know he's alive?"

"Very much," she agreed, a lump of emotion rising in her throat.

"Perhaps tomorrow," Rudi suggested. "He's — er — rather tired today."

"Oh, but — "

He shot a quelling look at Gabi, who fell silent.

29

"Whatever you think best," she acquiesced. "Kristal can have the room next to mine, can't she? Then we can talk girly things — just like sisters. You must stay at least a month. I love what you're wearing."

"I haven't brought much with me," Kristal informed her. "So my stay's rather limited, I'm afraid."

"You can borrow some of my clothes — we're the same size. Or we can go shopping — ".

"You've just been shopping," Rudi reminded her.

Gabi laughed. "I adore shopping," she confessed.

"Tell me about my — tell me about Gustav," Kristal asked.

"Poor Gustav is bored silly, most of the time. His mind's as active as ever, but he's terribly arthritic, and can't do most of the things he used to do, so he thinks up naughty little pranks."

"Like having his obituary printed in the Times!"

"Yes. It was a bit over the top,

30

I suppose, but he thought it hugely funny. Condolences poured in from all over the world. Dozens of people with the name von Steinberg claimed kinship, hoping to inherit. It kept him amused for days! A disclaimer was due to be published today, so we'll have to think up some other way to keep him amused."

"I know neither of you meant any harm, darling," Rudi told her fondly, and Kristal felt that nasty stabbing pain again, "but it was downright foolish of the pair of you. They have a mutual admiration society, Gustav and Gabi," he told Kristal.

He may not have intended to hurt her, but today, for some reason, Kristal felt ultra-sensitive. If Gustav had married Analiese, would she now be sharing a special relationship with Gustav herself? Would she be the darling of Rudi? Would she want to be?

The door opened and a thin, elderly woman walked in. Her feet made no sound on the carpeted floor. She had grey hair, drawn back severely from her pale, waxen face. The years had not been kind to her — there were no laughter lines in the papery skin, just a malevolent tension that showed in the tightly pursed mouth, the strange multi-coloured eyes, loaded with unspoken criticism, that lit on Kristal with suspicion.

"Aunt Mathilde! Guess what! We think we've found a distant cousin — isn't it marvellous?"

"I wasn't aware we had lost any," came the ready reproof.

"No, I made a mistake," Kristal said quickly. "I was about to leave."

"Till we persuaded her to stay." To Kristal's amazement, it was Rudi who spoke. "She'll be company for Gabi, and maybe liven up your brother."

So this was Gustav's sister, Mathilde. Kristal remembered Analiese talking about her, but she could not remember what her grandmother had said.

The malevolent eyes scrutinised Kristal

meticulously, till she felt distinctly uncomfortable.

"Whatever made you think you were related to us?" she said scornfully. "Where do you come from?"

"England."

The old lady was clearly disconcerted by her answer. "You're English?"

"Yes."

"Well, there you are, then."

"My grandmother was Austrian, though."

"This is intriguing — you must tell us all about it over dinner," Gabi enthused. "We'd better go up and change. She can have the room next to mine, can't she, Aunt Mathilde?"

"Why not?" the old lady replied, unable to think of a reason, though clearly wanting to.

★ ★ ★

Half an hour later, after finishing her bath with a cool shower and blow-drying her hair, Kristal felt clean and

33

refreshed. She stood in front of the mirror as the steam cleared, in just her underwear.

She was tall for a girl, and slender, but she had curves in all the right places — a firm, high bust and neatly rounded hips. In England she towered above most women — in fact, she towered above most people. Here in Austria, however, she had already noticed how much taller people were, both men and women. Analiese, at five feet eight, had been two inches shorter than herself. What would Gustav be like? Would he look like his tight-lipped stick of a sister, now slightly stooped, but still quite tall?

Her mind moved on, to thoughts of Rudi. He was six feet three inches of gorgeous muscle and bone. She remembered how it had felt to be held in his arms, and felt her body tingling at the memory. He didn't believe she was genuine. He clearly despised her, but he had been unexpectedly kind when she had felt faint, and had actually informed the sour Mathilde she was to stay. It was obvious that it was he who held sway in this household. Even Mathilde accepted his edicts, yet, Kristal thought with a shudder, left to Mathilde, she had a feeling she would be out on the street by now.

Why had Rudi capitulated about her staying? Was it because Gabi had wanted her to stay? Rudi was clearly very fond of her. Who could blame him? Gabi was the sort of girl Kristal could easily be friends with. They could each be the sister the other had never had.

As Kristal walked through to the bedroom there was a tap on her door and, without waiting for an answer, Gabi walked in.

"What do you think?" she asked, twirling round in a chiffon dress in hyacinth blue, the halter neck leaving her back bare, the pure lines of fitted bodice and flaring skirt making the most of her lovely figure.

"It's gorgeous! Is that what you're

wearing tonight?"

"I thought I might. I bought it today. It rather depends what you've brought —

I don't want to look overdressed."

"How about this?" Kristal asked, producing a black, crêpe dress. She pulled it on, adjusting its sleek lines to her slender hips. "Perfect! We don't dress up every night for dinner, though."

"That's a relief. My wardrobe's strictly limited. Why tonight?"

"Rudi's second-in-command at the bank, Andreas, is coming to dinner. Besides, we usually make it something of an occasion when we have guests. And you're here, of course, but I've already begun to think of you as family."

"You're very sweet, Gabi. Tell me, do your parents live here?"

"No." Gabi's eyes clouded over. "They died in a car accident when I was ten. That's when Rudi came to live here. He took Papa's place at the bank.

Now he's its president. He's also one of the most wonderful, dependable people I know. He and Opa have made sure I lack for nothing — except actually my parents."

"And Mathilde?"

"She can be a bit of a pain, but you'll get used to her."

"I shan't be here long enough," Kristal responded wryly.

"I hope you'll stay for ages."

"Well, I haven't taken a holiday in ages, so I do have four weeks due — "

"Good! So you can stay a month!"

"I'm not sure about that," Kristal said hesitantly. How would Rudi take it?

"You must — at least a month."

"A month maximum. After that, it's back to the grindstone."

"What do you do for a living?"

Kristal told her and they were still talking fashion when they went downstairs, having helped to do each other's hair. Gabi was wearing a necklet of lapis lazuli set in silver, while Kristal wore her one good piece of jewellery — a sapphire and diamond pendant that her grandmother had given her.

A murmur of male voices reached them as they approached the drawing-room. Like the rest of the house, this was lavishly decorated in pale, tasteful colours, with comfortable, gilt-framed seating arranged on a deep-pile carpet, its beautiful jewel colours gleaming with the sheen of silk. Subtle lighting came not from the chandeliers that hung from the ceiling, but from table-lamps and wall-sconces with finely-pleated, silk shades.

As they entered, the two men who had been conversing turned towards them. Kristal's eyes were drawn to Rudi, who looked incredibly elegant in evening attire. Beside him stood a man of almost the same height, but very fair, with pale-blue eyes. His formal dress was relieved by a waistcoat of rich peacock tones. They made an extraordinarily attractive duo.

"Rudi," Gabi greeted him, kissing him lightly. "Andreas!" she exclaimed, turning to the other man, reaching up to kiss his cheek.

Kristal could not help but notice the way Andreas's hands clasped Gabi's arms, holding her just long enough to return her kiss. She glanced at Rudi, who was watching the procedure objectively.

"Andreas, say hello to our new cousin — Kristal," Gabi demanded, laughing her tinkling laugh at Andreas's puzzlement.

"How do you do, Kristal?" he enquired politely.

As she returned his greeting, Kristal found her hand encompassed in both those of Andreas. They were nice hands, in fact, he was a remarkably good-looking man, yet she felt no quickening of her pulse, no desire to remain in contact, as she had earlier with Rudi.

"Would you like a sherry, Kristal?" Rudi asked her.

"Yes, please," she said, turning to smile her thanks, to find him scowling at her anew.

She turned away and Andreas immediately swung round from a silent exchange with Gabi. He was a very pleasant individual, around twenty-nine, at a guess — and he wasn't scowling.

"I understand you work with Rudi?" she said.

"For my sins, yes. I run the dealing room at the bank."

"That sounds interesting."

"The pace is incredibly fast." Gabi smiled. "I'll take you to see them at work."

"I can't see much work being done with you two there to disrupt things," Rudi commented drily.

"How can you say that?" Gabi protested, pouting playfully.

"How can he not?" Andreas teased. "You look quite stunning this evening, Gabi — as does your new cousin." He turned to Kristal and enquired, "And

40

which branch of the family do you spring from?"

"Yes, do tell us," Gabi begged.

"I suggest we leave those particular skeletons in the cupboard for now," Rudi said darkly.

"Skeletons? Ah! Some indiscretion on the part of a von Steinberg! Which one, I wonder. There have been so many indiscretions. Was it darling Opa?"

"I said leave it," Rudi snapped.

"Sorry," Gabi apologised with a puzzled frown. "You are an old grouch this evening, Rudi, darling."

Rudi downed a large whisky in one and crashed the glass down on a table.

"Let's go in to dinner, shall we? Gustav won't be joining us and Mathilde will be waiting."

"Why didn't she join us in here?" Kristal asked.

"She never does. At least, not when I'm here," Andreas informed her. "Can't think what she's got against me!"

"Don't be absurd, Andreas," Gabi said. "She's just against drinking before and after, as well as during, a meal, as you know very well."

"May I escort you in to dinner?" Andreas asked Kristal, crooking his elbow with a disarming smile.

"Danke schön," she thanked him.

"Bitte schön," he rejoined.

"The small dining-room?" he enquired of Rudi.

"Indeed."

Rudi's hand slid under Gabi's elbow. The glance he offered his companion was full of tenderness yet when he looked back at Kristal, there was condemnation in his eyes.

Mathilde was indeed waiting in the dining-room, sombre in grey silk, with pearls at her scrawny throat.

"Andreas, you will sit on Rudi's right, with our other guest beside you."

There was a meaningful silence of several seconds. It was a carefully calculated insult not to place Kristal, a female guest, to the right of her host in their very proper society. Kristal slid into her allotted place without a word.

"Good, now we can make plans for tomorrow," Gabi whispered, taking the end seat and leaning towards her.

Mathilde was sitting in the middle of the long side opposite Kristal and Andreas.

Andreas's natural good humour and fund of amusing anecdotes soon drew Rudi out of his dark mood. Gabi laughed with delighted unconcern as the men kept them entertained.

"Who would have thought banking could be so much fun?" Kristal commented, after one particular story from Andreas.

"Don't tell me nothing interesting ever happens in a fashion house!" Gabi challenged.

"We have our moments."

With that, Kristal embarked on some of the amusing incidents that had happened in her own sphere of work, which had Gabi and the menfolk in stitches. Not so Mathilde, though.

"I sometimes wish I had a career," Gabi said wistfully.

"Your job is to look decorative," Andreas declared.

"But Kristal manages that as well!"

"You're quite right, but you don't need to work — " He ran out of words.

"It's time you and Rudi set a date for the wedding," Mathilde announced.

"I'd no idea you were engaged," Kristal blurted out, wondering why the thought of Rudi marrying Gabi had suddenly made her feel sick inside.

"It's not absolutely decided," Gabi insisted quietly, serious for once.

"It's always been understood," Mathilde stated ominously. Kristal glanced towards Rudi and wondered at his unfathomable expression.

"Shall we adjourn for coffee?" he suggested.

"I'll have mine with Gustav," Mathilde said, to Kristal's relief.

That woman definitely didn't like

her, and the feeling was mutual. In fact, she gave Kristal the creeps! They all stood up and made for the door, reaching it at about the same time.

"Swap!" Gabi said, her good humour returned.

She took Andreas's arm and Kristal couldn't help but wonder at the intimate look that passed between them. No wonder Rudi was scowling as he offered his arm to her, when his future wife was flirting with his second-in-command.

"I feel like dancing!" Gabi declared, when coffee was dispensed with and the men were enjoying a brandy.

"I think we should show your English cousin just how the Viennese can waltz. Don't you?" Andreas suggested, rising to his feet. He went over to the hi-fi, discreetly placed in a corner, slid in a compact disc and set it turning.

"May I?" he asked, offering his hand to Gabi, but addressing the question to Rudi.

"Be my guest."

45

They looked superb together, the elegant, blond Austrian and his tall, graceful partner, her upswept, dark hair gleaming, as they waltzed to the strains of Strauss.

"Do you want to give it a try?" Rudi asked.

Kristal smiled her delight, turning her eyes to sapphires and she could have sworn that Rudi caught his breath.

"Don't forget my grandmother was also Viennese," she reminded him, going into his arms.

It was like coming home, reminding her as it did of his embrace a few hours ago when he had held her in his arms and kissed her. He was a wonderful dancer, executing with skill the steps which in themselves were so simple, yet required such grace and balance, such a sense of music, rhythm and gaiety.

Kristal glanced up and surprised a look of warm contentment on her partner's face.

"You dance very well," he conceded. "Shall we continue?"

46

"I'd like that."

They had circled the room twice more before Kristal noticed they were alone. As they turned she saw that a door to an adjoining room was open. Through it, she could see the other two deep in conversation, not dancing, but still loosely in each other's arms, as if they had only just stopped. The music drew to a close and Rudi changed the disc to one of a modern, slow tempo. He drew her once more into his arms.

"You look wonderful in black, little English cousin," he murmured.

She felt his breath against her hair. She didn't understand what was going on, only that she was in Rudi's arms and she never wanted to leave them. He gathered her closer and she felt the hard planes of his body against her own soft, pliant form.

"Should we be dancing like this?" she asked after a while.

"Why not? It's only a dance," he said huskily. "What harm are we doing?

Don't you like dancing with me?"

"Yes," she conceded shakily, yet it still made her feel guilty.

"Would you rather be in Andreas's arms?" he demanded darkly. "I saw the way you looked at him earlier."

"What way was that?"

"You were flirting with him!"

"I was not! Anyway, you're the one who's engaged," she reminded him.

"Just shut up and dance," he said softly, his expression closed.

But it wasn't exactly dancing, just moving against each other, Kristal's eyes drifting closed as she enjoyed being in his arms. He tilted her chin, forcing her to look up. His eyes were dark, a circle of gold around each huge pupil.

"I am very attracted to you, Kristal Hastings," he stated baldly.

She gasped. "B-but you're — "

"I know what you're going to say, but that doesn't alter the fact that I want you. Why shouldn't we enjoy your sojourn here together? The way

48

you say Analiese enjoyed herself with Gustav — ”

"Analiese and Gustav were in love!" Kristal hissed angrily, not wanting the others to hear. "And you're engaged to one of the sweetest girls I've ever met!"

"The engagement's unofficial. Having reached the age of thirty-four, I'm in no particular hurry to get married. If and when I do marry, I intend to be perfectly faithful. Meanwhile, there's no harm in having a little fun — ”

"You're absolutely despicable! I hate you, Rudi von Steinberg."

"Of course you do, because you know you can't pull the wool over my eyes, but you want me as much as I want you. You can't hide your response to me."

At that moment, Gabi and Andreas strolled leisurely back into the room, side by side, not touching. Kristal took a deep breath to compose herself.

"I'm just going up, Gabi. It's been a lovely evening."

"Andreas wants to rush off, too, but the night is still young!"

"Some of us have work to do in the morning," her companion reminded her.

"We'll see you out," Rudi said, his hand taking Kristal's elbow.

Andreas kissed both women on the cheek and shook Rudi's hand before disappearing into the night.

"Won't you stay up a little longer?" Gabi asked. "There's so much we have to talk about."

"There's always tomorrow, at breakfast — if you're up," Rudi put in.

"I'll try to be. I might as well go up and read," Gabi announced, somewhat to Kristal's surprise — after all, shouldn't she want to spend time alone with the man she was to marry? And such a man! "Good-night, Rudi, darling."

"Good-night, *liebchen*," Rudi replied, kissing her lightly on the cheek.

"Good-night, Kristal." Gabi kissed her cheek and started up the stairs.

Kristal moved to follow. "You haven't kissed our new cousin good-night, Rudi."

"No more I have," he replied, pulling Kristal away from the staircase. Looking daggers at him, she offered her cheek for the required kiss. "See you in the morning," Gabi called before disappearing along a corridor. Lean fingers turned Kristal's face to Rudi's. "You're very beautiful, with your sapphire eyes and yellow-gold hair," he said. Her eyes fell to his sensuous, mobile mouth, then, with a great effort of will, she turned away. It was no use trying to escape him — his lips touched the corner of her mouth and her legs turned to jelly. She wanted to be held and touched — she was too weak to stand alone.

As if he knew, he circled her waist with one arm, supporting her as his lips moved over hers. She clung to him, offering her mouth for more. He teased her, his lips sliding to kiss the smooth perfection of her cheekbones, her closed eyelids, before returning to her lips. He touched them briefly and drew away, looking deeply into her eyes.

The next instant his lips were on hers, cruelly plundering, offering no quarter, and just as suddenly it was over and she was free.

"Good-night, little English cousin," he said softly.

She stared up at him, flushed and dazed. When her brain cells started to function once more she uttered a little gasp and took off with unseemly haste up the stairs, to the soft laughter of her handsome, hateful cousin, Rudi. Halfway up she caught a movement on the gallery above. Was that the swish of grey silk fading into the darkness of the corridor beyond?

3

KRISTAL awoke the next morning feeling more in need of a night's sleep than when she had gone to bed. For half the night she had lain awake, disturbed by that final embrace. It was Rudi who openly admitted his desire, yet he had been the one able to pull away as if nothing had happened.

She had half a mind to pack her things and leave right away, without even meeting the man she believed to be her grandfather. He sounded half crazy, anyway, having his obituary inserted in the Times.

Yet if she left now she would be conceding defeat, allowing Rudi to believe her a liar, and she didn't want that. She didn't want him to think the worst of her. After all, what was she asking for? Nothing! She merely wanted to know that she was not alone

53

in the world, that she had a family somewhere, then she could go back and get on with her life. Couldn't she?

After taking a cool shower to wake herself up, she put on a cream linen dress, fixed her hair and added gold studs to her ears, then, looking more composed than she felt, she went downstairs.

A smiling Trudi directed her to the breakfast room, where, to her dismay, there was no Gabi, only Rudi, half hidden behind a newspaper and Mathilde. He mumbled a greeting. Mathilde nodded sourly in response to Kristal's pleasant good-morning, and carried on with her breakfast.

She approached the table uncertainly. Rudi glanced up, lowering the paper, and she noticed, with surprise, that he was wearing riding gear. There was a hint of understanding in the shadowed, amber eyes.

"Sit anywhere," he told her. "We don't stand on ceremony for breakfast."

With which, as she sat down and

accepted a cup of steaming coffee from Trudi, he disappeared once more behind his newspaper. Trudi went off in what she supposed was the direction of the kitchen.

Helping herself to a croissant, she addressed Mathilde.

"That was a splendid meal last night, Mathilde."

"You enjoyed dining here, did you?" came the unsmiling reply.

"I enjoyed the entire evening from start to finish," she assured the other woman defiantly, some little devil in her wanting to needle this rude, old woman.

"I'm sure you did."

With which Mathilde dabbed her thin, dry lips, pushed her chair back and walked out. Rudi lowered his paper and she saw his chest shaking with laughter.

"People usually find Mathilde intimidating," he told her. "You've given her something to think about — especially as she's just torn a strip off me for

55

saying a rather too enthusiastic good-night to you."

"Good for her."

"You've just admitted you enjoyed it — I'm glad," he said smugly.

"I was excluding the last bit."

"Liar. When you've finished eating, I'll take you up to see Gustav."

"Oh, will you really?"

Her animosity fled, her eyes shining, her heart thudding at the thought of at last meeting the man she had heard so much about from darling Analiese. What a bonus to find the man still alive. Their joke may have been sick, but without it, she would not be here at all. Gustav's room faced south looking out over the garden at the back of the house, which Kristal had yet to explore. There was a figure silhouetted against the window, sitting in a high-backed chair, a folding table with the remains of his breakfast in front of him. He looked up as they entered.

"Good-morning, Rudi." His glance switched to Kristal "And whom do we have here?"

He peered towards her. She had stopped, suddenly shaky in the presence of a man she had believed dead, a man whom her grandmother had loved, but who had rejected her. She was swept by an ambivalence of feelings: love, hate, curiosity, indifference. Rudi's hand at her elbow propelled her forward.

"Gustav is short-sighted, but he refuses to wear his glasses till after breakfast, in the belief that it will strengthen his sight. Kristal saw your obituary, Gustav, and came all the way from England to meet the rest of the family."

They were a few feet away now. Gustav was sitting stiffly upright, a big man like Rudi, but slightly shrunken with age. He had a proud, noble face, with wonderful bone structure, the grey eyes bright and intelligent. It was not difficult to believe that, in his youth, he would have been a very attractive man.

Kristal was beginning to feel strange to be meeting him at last. She shook her head to clear it, unaware of how her hair was catching the reflected fingers of sunlight that streamed in through the window beside her.

"Mein Gott! Her hair is just like — "

"Just like what, Gustav?" came Rudi's hard, uncompromising voice.

"Only once before have I seen such pure gold, like sunlight on wind-ruffled water. Ah, but she was beautiful, my Analiese."

A sob rose in Kristal's throat. So, he had not forgotten her grandmother.

"Analiese? Who was this Analiese, Gustav?" Rudi demanded.

"The most beautiful girl in the world — and the most treacherous. I thought she had given me her heart, but she turned out to be a shallow creature, out for a good time. She left me, and I married Elfrieda, the staid but reliable Elfrieda."

"Analiese was my grandmother," Kristal announced, ignoring the warning pressure of Rudi's fingers locking cruelly round her upper arm.

Gustav leaned forward. "You're — Then that explains your beautiful hair. What became of her, Kristal? What happened after she walked out on me?"

"She made for England, and married an Englishman," Rudi informed him. "David Hastings, wasn't it?"

He addressed the question to Kristal, who glanced up to meet the mocking triumph on his face, for how could she deny it?

"I told you exactly how that came about."

"So you did."

Gustav took in their exchange with interest.

"Pass me my glasses, Rudi." He slid on the dark-framed glasses and peered up at Kristal. She gazed steadily back.

"Yes, Analiese's hair, but those eyes! As blue as my mother's. Isn't that

59

amazing? As blue as Gabi's, too. Incredible!"

"Come on, Gustav! The majority of people in Austria have blue eyes."

Gustav ignored him, asking, "Do you play chess, Kristal?"

She gave him one of her wide smiles. "Rather well, actually."

"Ah, such a smile. Will you come up and play with me some time?"

"Of course. We could play now, if you like. Gabi isn't about yet, and I'm sure Rudi has work to do."

"The chess will have to wait — Gustav and I have some business to discuss."

"I'll see you later then, Gustav," she said and winked at him. "I'm delighted the obituary was a hoax."

She received a conspiratorial smile in return.

"Not as delighted as I am, my dear. Now then, Rudi — "

She let herself quietly out of the room, wondering what to do next.

"There you are!" Gabi exclaimed, hurrying towards her and linking her

60

arm through Kristal's. "So you've met darling Opa. What do you think of him?"

"He's terrific. Mind you, I hope to spend more time with him and get to know him better. He and Rudi are discussing business right now."

"Yes, he likes to keep his finger on the pulse — it keeps him young, in mind, if not in body. Rudi's taking us into Vienna this morning."

"Wonderful! Any special reason?"

"You don't need a reason to go to Vienna. Vienna is a reason."

Johann chauffeured them in the long, black Mercedes but, when they reached the city, Gabi suddenly remembered a friend she had promised to call on, to discuss a charity ball. Kristal felt both abandoned yet strangely excited to be left alone with Rudi.

"Show her the sights," was Gabi's parting order.

"I can easily get a plan of the city and see the sights for myself," she offered when they were alone.

"Gabi would never forgive me. She's taken a liking to you."

He was a splendidly entertaining and informative guide. Johann drove them hither and thither while Rudi pointed out places of interest, eventually taking her to St Stephen's Cathedral.

As they walked away from the car towards the blue-tiled cathedral she could hear the sound of singing from within. Sweet, high voices, like a heavenly choir.

"The Vienna Boys' Choir?" she asked, entranced.

"Exactly! One of them, that is. There are three, one based here in Vienna, one that tours Austria, and a third that travels the world. It's considered a great honour to join the choir."

They let themselves into the cathedral, where the sound swelled to fill every corner of the beautiful building. The choir stalls were filled with well-scrubbed choirboys in cassocks and ruffs, their mostly blond heads gleaming, earnest eyes lifted to the choirmaster's baton.

Kristal stood still, rivetted to the spot; letting the sound expand to fill her mind and soul.

Analiese had told her of the choir, and how she had come here in her youth to hear its rehearsals, as they were doing now. The united voices were holding and extending a final note, letting it gradually fade away. The choirmaster issued some instructions, the organ sounded and they began to sing once more. It was the Panus Angelicus, a favourite of Analiese's. As the pure voices soared in unison, tears filled Kristal's eyes and ran unheeded down her cheeks. She found herself gently shepherded towards one of the polished pews, where Rudi took her hand in his as she sat down. Her fingers curled round his, seeking the comfort he offered.

After that song, the choir began to shuffle about, taking a break, becoming just another group of normal schoolboys.

"Why did that make you cry?" he

asked softly as they wandered round, examining the stained-glass windows among the many interesting features.

"It was one of my grandmother's favourites."

"I'm sorry — I tend to forget your loss is so recent."

His arm went around her shoulders and stayed there till they were out in the spring sunshine once more.

After a delightful trip in a horse-drawn trap around the old, cobbled streets of Vienna, they met Gabi, as arranged, for lunch, in a very exclusive-looking restaurant. Gabi was already there, having a drink at the bar.

They were soon seated round a low table enjoying an apéritif together.

"We often lunch here," Rudi told her once the waiter had taken their orders.

It ought not to have been surprising, therefore, when Andreas joined them.

"I thought I might find you here," he told Rudi. "Don't forget, you have some appointments in the office, this afternoon."

"I wasn't planning on being out of the office all day," he replied wryly. "I've enjoyed this morning, however. One rarely plays tourist in one's own city."

Was that the only reason, Kristal wondered with a stab of disappointment. She had enjoyed the tour, very much so, but her pleasure had been more than doubled by having Rudi beside her as escort.

"How did your morning go, *liebchen*?" Rudi asked Gabi.

"Very well, darling. We've decided on a venue for the ball, at least."

"Well, that's a start. Where's it to be?"

"At the von Steinberg residence," she informed him mischievously.

"Oh, no!" Rudi's hands went up as if to ward off some disaster. "I'm not having the place turned upside down by a load of drunken revellers!"

"But, darling, I've said it's all right. And anyway, the tickets will be enormously expensive, and by

65

invitation only — it's not as if we're opening the doors to all and sundry."

"Gabi, this is the twentieth century, but loutish, drunken behaviour has never been the perogative of the poor. It just happens in different venues, that's all."

"Darling, don't be difficult. After all, it is my home, too. Don't you think the house would be just perfect for a charity ball, Kristal?"

"Leave me out of this," she begged laughingly.

"But you could help me organise it. I'll bet you're marvellous at organising things." Gabi turned, once more, to Rudi. "Don't be stuffy. Think what fun it would be, and Opa could come down for a while — he'd love it."

Rudi looked from one girl's face to the other. Kristal said nothing, but he couldn't fail to notice how interesting she found the idea.

"Very well, Gabi, but I shall hold you personally responsible for any losses or breakages — it will come out of your allowance."

"Oh, I do love you!" she cried, half standing to kiss him on the lips.

Once again Kristal felt that stab of jealousy. Her eyes lit on Andreas for an instant, to surprise a bleak misery in his. There was no doubt about it — Andreas was in love with the impulsive Gabi. It seemed both men were, and who could blame them? She was such a happy creature.

After lunch the men returned to the bank while Johann drove the girls home.

"I must go up and see Op — your grandfather when we get back," Kristal said on the way. "I promised him a game of chess."

"He'll like that," Gabi replied. "I'll come, too, if that's all right."

4

AS chess opponents, Kristal and Gustav were pretty evenly matched. The game, therefore, became a matter of will between two keenly-tuned minds, each trying to gain ascendancy over the other. Gabi sat quietly watching, but not near enough to prove a distraction.

The game was drawing to a close, with only a few pieces left on the board, and Kristal was daring to hope she stood a chance of winning. There was no question of either letting the other win. She glanced away briefly, meeting Gabi's eyes, and surprised in them an unexpected glimpse of sadness. It proved Kristal's undoing, sidetracking her from the game at a strategic moment. She made her next move and it was all over — Gustav had won.

He chortled with glee. "I didn't expect you to give the game away like that," he told her, mirthfully. "I thought you'd got it in the bag."

"So did I! Which just goes to show — you shouldn't count your chickens before they're hatched! Are you all right, Gabi?"

"Of course!" Though her laughter was a little forced. "I wish I could play chess," she added wistfully.

"You've never wanted to before." Gustav frowned. "I would have been happy to teach you, *liebchen*. I still can, but why now?"

"Because you obviously enjoy it so much. You must get tired of my endless prattle." She sighed. "I don't do anything really useful. Not like Kristal. She holds down a responsible job, she speaks our language like a native — "

"Which my grandmother was, don't forget — she and I often talked in German, especially towards the end."

"Tell me about Analiese — was she happy with her English husband?"

69

Gustav asked huskily. "Is he still alive?"

"No, I'm afraid he's dead," she admitted. "She never married again."

"Kristal!"

She hadn't heard Rudi enter the room and started at the sound of her name.

"I'd like a word with you, right away, Kristal," he barked at her.

She shrugged and followed him from the room, aware of the curious eyes behind her. Rudi strode ahead to a room at the end of the corridor.

Beyond the doorway lay an obviously masculine room filled with solid pieces of furniture, large land and sea-scapes in oils on pale, stark walls, and a vast, carved four-poster standing squarely in the centre. It just had to be Rudi's.

"I'm not in the habit of going into men's bedrooms alone," she declared.

Lean fingers closed round her wrist and yanked her inside.

"You're not alone — you're with me!"

He closed the door and turned to face her, removing his jacket which he threw on a chair nearby. His tie went next.

"Excuse me, but if you're about to perform a striptease, I'd like you to know it's a form of entertainment that leaves me cold."

"Is that a fact? Well, don't worry, this is as far as it goes."

"You said you wanted a word," she reminded him.

"I want to know what sob story you were feeding Gustav. There's no way I'm going to allow you to usurp Gabi's position, so you can forget all this nonsense about Gustav and Analiese."

"It's not nonsense, and I didn't bring up the subject — he did. Why shouldn't he wonder about what happened to her, even if he had her thrown out? Maybe he regrets it. And you needn't worry — I'm not after Gabi's inheritance, just her friendship. She'll be the same rich heiress when you marry her as she is now."

"Are you suggesting I'd marry Gabi for her money?"

"N-not entirely," she admitted as his fingers closed cruelly about her upper arms. "B-but you can hardly be marrying her for love!"

"Why not?" he demanded softly, jerking her hard against him.

"Because if you did love her, you wouldn't be interested in another woman. I'm sure Gabi would prefer a faithful husband."

"We're not married yet. Of course I love Gabi. I've always loved her, but there are different kinds of love."

His dark, handsome head lowered towards hers, his eyes glittering with fury and passion. She struggled to avoid his lips but his fingers tightened about her arms. The more she struggled the closer he pulled her towards him.

With a moan of despair she clutched his shoulders, lifting her lips to his. His mouth descended to hers, and the more he demanded, the more she gave, one hand about his neck, her fingers sliding into the thick darkness of his hair. Her other hand ran over the muscles of his chest, that tensed against her touch.

Her head arched backwards as he moved his lips gently over her throat. His fingers, so cruel about her arms now gentled on her tender curves, his lips tracing a path of agonising sweetness across her shoulders.

She murmured his name, over and over again.

He lifted his head, his amber eyes glittering. The next moment he had hoisted her into his arms and carried her to the bed, lowering her on to it and following her down, his body half covering her own. His lips sought hers again more urgently and she clung to him . . .

A harsh sound intruded, bursting the bubble of enchantment enclosing them both. The phone rang, shrill and unreal, through the haze of their desire. Rudi's oath could be understood in any language as he reached for the phone.

"Yes!" he snapped. "What is it,

Andreas?" He listened intently, leaning against the pillow. Then he quickly sat up, turning his back on her, shutting her out. "That three-way currency deal? What's the problem? Look, come round for dinner — we'll discuss the best course of action, then. I have a few ideas."

While he concluded the call, Kristal slid off the bed the other side, shakily smoothing down her dress and putting her appearance to rights. Rudi put down the receiver and stood up, turning to face her.

"You've had a narrow escape. You won't get away so easily next time."

"There won't be a next time," she muttered. "Just keep your hands off me."

"I can't seem to help myself," he replied, as if the fact surprised him. "Just remember what I said about Gustav. He's an old man. I won't have him upset."

"I don't intend to upset him. In fact, I could easily grow very fond of him."

"How convenient!" he sneered. "You'd better run along now."

With a little cry, she fled back to the relative safety of her own room.

* * *

Rudi concluded his business with Andreas before the meal began and when they sat down to eat, they were in very good spirits, the problem at the bank obviously dealt with to their satisfaction.

Kristal could hardly be unaware, however, of the various undercurrents that flowed between the group — the brief, hungry glances Andreas gave to Gabi. There was a certain preoccupation beneath the usual, unfailing cheerfulness of the dark-haired girl.

Rudi's dark gaze held a glow of passion and an unmistakable glint of triumph, as if he had already possessed Kristal.

Then there was Mathilde, unfailingly spiteful and malevolent, her every comment subtly informing Kristal that there was no place for her in their household, and certainly not with Rudi.

"Has Rudi told you we're having a charity ball right here?" Gabi demanded of Mathilde. "Kristal's going to help me to organise it. Aren't you, Kristal?"

"If you think I can help, Gabi."

"Of course you can! I've decided it will be a masked ball — I thought we'd all dress up in mid-nineteenth-century costume. What do you think, Rudi?"

"Well, if it's that or a bunch of gorillas and Roman centurions, then I would prefer it, I must say."

"Good, then that's settled. We'll have it about ten days from now, if we can hire an orchestra in time."

"No problem," Andreas said. "Would you like me to hire one? I have several contacts who might help."

"Oh, would you, Andreas? That would be very sweet of you."

"If it's so soon, we'd better see a printer tomorrow, to get the invitations done," Kristal put in. "You did say by invitation only, didn't you?"

"Yes, I did, Kristal. Rudi, darling, can we use the bank's printers? I'm sure they could come up with some stunning design."

"Of course, *liebchen*. Just let them know what you want."

"Prima!" she exclaimed with delight.

"Perhaps you could help Gabi to draw up a list of guests, Mathilde," Kristal suggested tentatively. The older woman looked startled.

Perhaps she would be more pleasant to have around if she were included in their plans, Kristal reasoned. She was quite certain that if Gabi invited those whom Mathilde did not consider the right people then she, Kristal, would be the one held responsible, by both Mathilde and Rudi.

"I'll draw up a list after I've said good-night to Gustav. Excuse me."

When Kristal glanced up Rudi was nodding his head slightly, whether in approval or because he had guessed her reasoning, she did not know, but she had a pretty good idea it was the latter. The wretched man seemed to read her mind, but did he know it was him she wanted to please most of all? Though why that should be, even she did not understand.

"What shall we do now?" Gabi demanded into the silence, and without waiting for an answer, declared, "I know! Let's take Kristal to the Prater Park."

"Now?" Rudi asked, barely disguising the dismay of a man who had a hard day's work behind him, and another to face in the morning.

"Darling, don't — "

"If you tell me not to be stuffy again, Gabi, *liebchen*, I shall be tempted to put you across my knee."

Gabi's initial astonishment was followed by a gale of laughter.

"I wasn't going to say any such thing, Rudi, darling. I was merely going to say don't come if you don't feel up to it — I'm quite sure Andreas would escort us."

Rudi's eyes narrowed, his shoulders shaking with laughter. "You, young lady, are incorrigible. It would seem I have no option but to come. I can't have you leading my second-in-command astray!"

Dusk was just falling when they arrived at the park. The four of them wandered along as a group, so that Kristal found herself talking at various times to Andreas, Gabi or Rudi, beneath trees threaded with lights, and past cafés from which emerged the sounds of Strauss and Lehar, the notes lingering on the balmy night air.

"How you Viennese love your own composers!" she commented to Andreas.

"But why not? Do they not contain that essential element of gaiety and flippancy that characterises the Viennese?"

"I don't see you as flippant."

"Perhaps that was a poor choice of word, but we do like to enjoy ourselves, and we have so much to enjoy in our city — culturally, artistically, visually.

Wherever you look, beauty meets your eyes."

He glanced pointedly at Gabi then at herself, a gesturing hand reinforcing his meaning. Both men were displaying commendable gallantry, each managing to hide the fact that Gabi was their preferred companion, but at his words, Rudi, who was just behind with Gabi, and whose ears must surely be ultra-sensitive, met Kristal's amused eyes with a scowl of disapproval.

"Flirtation is a favourite Viennese pastime," he informed her, "but one which can be dangerous."

Gabi had pulled Andreas away to watch a wandering busker and Kristal now found herself next to Rudi, once again.

Stalls selling everything from hot-dogs to souvenirs grew increasingly numerous as they approached the funfair, which was dominated by the famous Ferris wheel. An ear-splitting cacophony of sound assaulted their ears, a total contrast to the cheerfully sedate cadences of the café orchestras.

Unable to talk without shouting, Kristal gave up trying. As she looked round, she noticed the four of them were attracting curious eyes, seeing four exquisitely beautiful people, one couple, for she was again beside Andreas, crowned with gold, the other dark as night. She was proud to be with the three Austrians — she almost felt a sense of belonging. Gabi was obviously having a friendly argument with Rudi, and from their gestures he was losing the battle to enjoy — or endure — a ride on the nearby carousel. With a resigned shrug he helped Gabi up and turned to Kristal, but she had already accepted Andreas's hand, to Rudi's scowling disapproval.

"That was brilliant!" Gabi yelled above the surrounding noise, when the ride was over and they had all climbed down.

She clutched Kristal's arm, leading her firmly towards the massive Ferris wheel, leaving the men to follow.

"Oh, no! You're not getting me on that thing!" Kristal declared.

"You can't come to the Prater and not go on the wheel!" Gabi laughed.

The gondolas were slowly filling up, disgorging their previous occupants. As each gondola was filled, the wheel moved on gracefully, pausing as the next one reached the landing stage. They were impelled forward by the surging crowd.

Rudi climbed aboard and Kristal waited for Gabi to join him, but instead, she found herself helped aboard, a hand at either elbow. She landed beside Rudi. She tried to leave, but the official closed the gondola door, trapping her.

"Sorry," she apologised, knowing Rudi would have wanted Gabi's company.

"I'm sure you are," he replied, "but you'll just have to put up with me."

The wheel revolved slowly. As it did so, they were presented with an amazing panorama of the city and its environs. Rudi pointed out the various sights around them, an arm about her shoulders and leaning close as he did so.

"There's the Danube, and over there the Donau Kanal," he said, pointing to the stretch of black water encircling the city, reflected lights shimmering in its surface. "You can see quite a lot of the Ringstrasse from up here, too."

She looked down on the wide road cutting a swath round Vienna and still teeming with traffic.

"There's the harbour," he whispered, his face close to hers. "Don't you sometimes have an urge to climb aboard a ship and sail off into the blue?"

There was something in his tone that made her realise it was not just an idle question.

"Is that what you would like to do?" she asked softly.

"Sometimes the weight of respon-sibilities becomes too much to bear alone," he surprised her by confiding, and she knew with sudden certainty that the cheerful, light-hearted Gabi would probably not lessen that burden. "Well?"

"Oh." She drew her thoughts back to his original question. "I think most of my life I've felt quite the reverse — like a ship adrift at sea, longing for an anchor."

With one lean finger he tilted her face to his, and saw the sincerity of her words reflected in her eyes. It was a feeling from deep in her heart which she was perhaps unwise to reveal.

"Poor Kristal," he murmured. "But I've offered you a temporary shelter from life's storms. Why do you reject me?"

"Perhaps it's because it is only temporary," she replied.

"We'd be good together, you and I," he murmured, and in the semi-darkness his lips sought hers and she shivered in his arms with desire.

"You're cold," he whispered. "We'll have coffee when we return to earth."

How mundane! The trouble was Kristal was unlikely to return to earth at all, for she knew, with absolute certainty, that she had fallen hopelessly and head-over-heels in love with Rudi.

Before their ride was over he had pointed out other landmarks: the airport with the occasional plane zooming in, lights flashing, to land on the runway. St Stephen's blue-tiled roof was lit up now, and, on one side of the city, was the dark, exciting shadow of the Vienna Woods, the Wienerwald.

"I have a hunting lodge in the Woods," he told her. "That's my real home."

"I thought the von Steinberg residence was your home."

"I moved in there shortly after Gabi's parents died. Gustav thought it would be a good idea — the house seemed so empty when they were gone. I'd given up my job to work at the bank by then, anyway, so Gustav and I were able to discuss business matters, which were new to me, at home. I had a lot to learn, though I'm not sure I enjoy thinking about banking morning, noon and night."

She wondered fleetingly whether Andreas was taking advantage of his time with Gabi, and whether it was what Gabi wanted, realising with a pang of guilt that this was the first time she had spared a thought for the other two since they had forced her into this gondola. When she was with Rudi he filled her heart and mind, and that was foolish — all he wanted, as he had just unequivocally stated, was a little light relief, and there was no way she intended to oblige.

5

IN the days that followed, Gabi introduced Kristal to the delights of shopping in Vienna. The latter was quickly seduced by the quality and variety of clothes on offer. Never had buying clothes been such fun for Kristal — Gabi was truly like a sister to her, and Gabi assured her she felt the same.

Preparations for the masked ball went by with scarcely a hitch. Andreas proved a tower of strength; his every phone call or visit brought a fund of new suggestions — for the authenticity of the staff's uniforms, the provision of flowers for the ballroom or the music itself. There was nothing the man didn't think of. He was as thoughtful as — well, a man in love, Kristal was quick to discern. True to his word, he engaged a first-rate orchestra, usually to be heard in one of Vienna's finest hotels.

"When I told them the ball was in aid of children's charities, they decided to waive their fee," he told the girls triumphantly.

"That's marvellous!" Gabi enthused. "And I've located a fabulous costumier, who can supply period costumes for the guests."

It was Saturday afternoon, and Kristal was disappointed that Rudi had not joined them.

Gabi turned to her now to ask, "Are you including a note about costumes with the invitations, Kristal?"

"Yes." She took out a packet of the gold-embossed, cream cards that Rudi had had printed. "They're very elegant, aren't they?"

"Perfect!" Gabi declared.

"What a pity Rudi had to work today," Kristal said lightly.

"Oh, he's probably escaped to his rotten, old hunting-lodge. He always does, given the chance," Gabi bemoaned.

"He does?" She remembered then that he had not always lived here, had not always worked at the bank. "What kind of job did he used to do?"

"He was Professor of History at the university," Andreas informed her. "A very good one, too. Whatever Rudi does, he does well — their loss has certainly been our gain."

"And he's still working on his 'Definitive History of the Hapsburg Empire'," Gabi quoted. "Which is probably what he's doing at this moment."

"No, he isn't," the deep voice of the man himself said. He had entered the room quietly and now slumped with a tired sigh on to the sofa next to Kristal. "I came home for a break before this evening. I've got four tickets for 'Die Fledermaus', if you three are interested."

"Oh, you clever thing! I heard it was fully booked," Gabi exclaimed excitedly.

"Yes, well, I got first option on cancellations."

"You enjoy opera?" Andreas enquired of Kristal.

"Very much, and 'Die Fledermaus' is one of my favourites — such happy music. Only four tickets — does that mean Mathilde won't be coming? I mean, won't she object to being left alone all evening?" she enquired.

"Not in the least," Rudi replied. "She always goes to bed early, but, in any case, she'll have Gustav's company this evening — he has decided to join us for dinner. He sometimes does, when his arthritis is not bothering him too much."

"That'll be nice," Kristal said.

She saw far too little of her grandfather, though she went up at least twice a day, sometimes to play chess, sometimes to listen to his reminiscences of the old days in Vienna, before the war, when he had been a young man. Once, he had asked her to take him down to the garden, in his wheel-chair, laughing at her puzzled expression.

"There's a lift opposite my door," he had explained. "It used to be a service shaft, but we had it enlarged, so that I can get about when I feel up to it."

He was, in fact, quite independent, propelling himself into the lift, and out on to the ground floor below, using ramps that had been specially installed to allow him access to the garden.

It was the first time Kristal had set foot in the garden. They had gone down a path under arches which in a few short weeks would be clustered with roses. In the centre of the garden a cool fountain splashed into a round pond where there was an occasional flash of gold or black beneath the lily-pads. The clean lines of late, spring flowers filled borders edging neatly-trimmed lawns.

Kristal and Gustav had sat on a seat overlooking the pond, talking companionably in the late spring sunshine, so still that birds almost fluttered to their feet, seeking insects that lurked among the pebbles.

★ ★ ★

"What are you going to wear?" Gabi asked now as they went upstairs to change for the evening ahead.

"The jade taffeta I bought the other day, I think. How about you?"

"The midnight blue I bought at the same time, I think."

Kristal's dress had a collar that stood high at the back, forming an Elizabethan-type ruff, but plunged low at the front. Gabi's was cut straight across her breasts, with long, fitted sleeves that were barely attached to the dress. They went downstairs together, made up and coiffured, perfumed and bejewelled, in a rustle of taffeta and silk.

"My! Aren't we privileged!" Rudi exclaimed. "You both look fantastic. Don't you agree, Andreas?"

"Fantastisch!" Andreas agreed, smiling with approval at Kristal, but reserving a special warmth for Gabi.

"You both look pretty good, too," Kristal said lightly, addressing her words to Andreas. "Don't you think, Gabi?"

"They'll do," she agreed, with a laugh.

The cancelled tickets Rudi had secured turned out to be an expensive box to the left of the stage. Gabi elected to sit nearest the stage. Rudi took the seat next to her so that Kristal found herself wedged between him and Andreas. She suspected Andreas would have preferred to change places with Rudi, but propriety would have frowned on that arrangement. The engagement understood between Gabi and Rudi was probably common knowledge in Viennese society.

Nothing could detract from the beauty of the lavish costumes and scenery, nor from the exquisite voices of both principals and chorus. It was a magical evening, altogether. During the interval, champagne was brought, and other members of the audience wandered in, having recognised them from the stalls. Conversation sparkled in an atmosphere of hedonistic pleasure, and any animosity between Rudi and Kristal was set aside for the evening.

There was genuine warmth, in fact, in the dark eyes that sometimes met hers. Perhaps they were reaching a new understanding. Kristal felt he had revealed a little of his heart to her that night at the Prater, while she had divulged something of herself to him, for which he had not as yet found cause to castigate her.

She woke early the following morning and, since the sun had been up for some time she showered, pulled on some jeans and a sweater and decided to go for a walk.

About to let herself out of the back door she heard footsteps behind her. Turning, she came face to face with Rudi, resplendent in riding gear, the tweed jacket filled by broad shoulders, the jodhpurs clinging to his muscled thighs.

"Where are you going?" he demanded quietly, as if reluctant to wake the rest of the household.

"I thought I'd take a walk."

"Couldn't sleep?" His voice was mocking.

"I slept very well — I just woke early, that's all. It seems too nice a day to laze about in bed."

"I agree. Come for a ride."

She spread her arms, looking down at her simple sweater and jeans, and ordinary walking shoes.

"You just need a jacket. Here." He reached one down from a peg near the door. "This is Gabi's. She won't mind if you borrow it."

"Well, if you're sure." She smiled, the prospect of a ride with Rudi very appealing. "How about a hat?"

"There are helmets in the stable," he said, guiding her through the doorway.

Johann was there before them, leading

out a huge and very frisky-looking, black stallion.

"Good-morning, Johann. Hello, Schwarzi."

Rudi stroked the muzzle of the huge beast, nodding its head up and down in delight at the sight of its master.

"Could you saddle up Gretel, Johann?"

"Of course."

While he was doing that, Rudi tethered an impatient Schwarzi and took Kristal round to meet the other horses. There were half a dozen, including a young foal, a creamy-blonde colour, a few months old, stabled with her mother.

"This is the newest addition to the stable," he told her proudly.

"She's beautiful," Kristal said, stroking the soft muzzle. "What's her name?"

"Blondie," he replied wryly. "Not very original, I'm afraid."

"She's absolutely perfect."

"Perhaps I should call her Kristal," he said contemplatively.

She glanced up sharply. His dark features were revealed in all their chiselled beauty in the clear, morning air, and he was looking down at her as if she, too, deserved the attribute of perfection. She laughed to dispel the tension that stretched between them.

Clattering hooves on the cobbles behind them drew their locked eyes to the grey mare, now saddled and ready.

"That was quick, Johann. I hope she's securely saddled."

"As always," Johann replied. "Here's your helmet, Rudi, and I think this one may fit the lady."

Kristal took the hard, metal helmet and tried it on. Having fastened his own, Rudi turned to fix the chin strap of hers.

"That's fine, Johann, thanks."

Johann left them, so he didn't see the pink flush that crept over Kristal's cheeks as Rudi's lean fingers inevitably stroked the satin flesh of her neck and chin as he secured the strap.

She carefully averted her gaze from his wonderful amber eyes but, having finished, he tilted her face to his and lowered his head to brush his lips across hers. It was only the briefest of kisses, but it sparked off little fireworks of pleasure that leaped and danced around her system.

"Come on," he murmured.

They rode for nearly an hour through the dark forest of the Vienna woods, lit here and there by shafts of the bright, morning sun through the trees. They had passed a few dwellings tucked away in its depths, but now they reached a large, stone-built house, in its own walled enclosure.

Rudi stopped, and Kristal paused beside him, enquiringly. He dismounted and took her reins, tethering both horses and turning to catch her as she jumped down. For an instant he held her against him and she inhaled a heady mixture of tweed and cologne.

"Come on," he said, turning away and cupping her elbow.

"Come where?"

"To see my home — I'm inviting you in for coffee."

This was his hunting lodge, and she had imagined one of those small, stone structures guarding the driveway to many an English country home. A sturdy door under the porch, set in a sheltered angle of the house burst open at that moment. A woman in her late fifties stood there wearing a welcoming smile, while two labradors, one cream, the other black, bounded out to greet them, barking loudly and wagging their tails.

"Come and meet Meggi. Down, Raben. Down, Honig. Hello, Meggi, how are you, today?"

Kristal soon learned that Meggi, Rudi's housekeeper, was Johann's mother. She and her late husband had always worked for Rudi's family, Kristal was told, and she had been the natural choice of housekeeper when her husband died. The house was comfortable and inviting, with discreetly-placed radiators that added warmth, without detracting from the character of oak-panelled walls and ancient, stone-flagged floors covered in bright, oriental rugs.

"You'll stay for breakfast?" Meggi enquired.

"We'd love to," Rudi replied.

The housekeeper lost no time in producing hot coffee, made from freshly-milled beans, fruit juice, and an assortment of rolls and croissants from the deep-freeze, together with curls of butter and home-made preserves. She served the meal in a huge, homely kitchen that owed nothing to modern high-tech and everything to solid beech fitments, though, as Meggi moved about the kitchen, Kristal glimpsed many modern gadgets behind reassuring facades.

"I can see why Rudi likes coming here." She smiled at the housekeeper, as she took her place at the large, scrubbed table. "You obviously spoil him."

"He deserves a bit of spoiling," came the reply.

It was obvious that, in Meggi's eyes, Rudi could do no wrong. Not that Kristal had any desire to criticise him — she was too busy enjoying her breakfast after their early-morning ride, and Rudi's unusually mellow company. After they had eaten, he pushed his chair back and stood up.

"I'm afraid we can't stay, Meggi. Johann told me to let you know he'll be here in good time for lunch. Thanks for the breakfast."

"Yes," Kristal added. "Thanks, Meggi — it was delicious."

"You're welcome," the pleasant housekeeper replied.

"Come on, Kristal. We must get back — we're expected in church."

"Are we expected in church?" Kristal enquired as they started back, disappointed to be leaving the old house.

"We always go," he informed her. "You don't want to get in Mathilde's bad books, do you?"

She met the gleam of amusement in his eyes and told him, "I don't have to try to do that. She doesn't like me at all."

"No," he mused contemplatively, not bothering to disagree.

The first person they met as they re-entered the kitchen of the von Steinberg residence was Mathilde herself. Kristal could not disguise the glow of good health colouring her cheeks, nor the sparkle in her eyes caused by the exhilarating ride back through the forest alongside the man she loved. Her spirits now took a dive seeing Mathilde's sour face.

"Where have you been, Rudi? Gustav's been asking for you," she snapped.

Rudi's smile broadened; he bent to kiss Mathilde's wrinkled cheek.

"We've had a wonderful ride through the woods," he replied. "As I often do on a Sunday."

"I know *you* do," she replied meaningfully.

"I'll go up and see what Gustav wants. Be ready for church in twenty minutes," he said to Kristal as he walked out of the room.

Before she could escape, Mathilde turned on her.

"Don't think I don't know what you're up to," she hissed venomously. "*She* was like you. You won't get him any more than she got my brother!"

The cook bustled in at that moment, her ruddy face beaming, unaware of the undercurrents passing between the two women in her kitchen. Kristal stared back at Mathilde for a moment then, deciding it wasn't worth a stand-up fight over something that was in the past and something else that was not likely to happen, she hurried away to shower again before dressing soberly for church.

Nevertheless, she pondered Mathilde's words. It was becoming increasingly clear that she hadn't liked Analiese, and it could be from that that her hatred of Kristal sprang. Gustav appeared to recall Analiese with fondness, whereas Mathilde obviously felt as venomous about her as about Kristal herself. Could Mathilde have had a hand in Analiese's dismissal?

During the sermon, Kristal's thoughts strayed to her morning ride with Rudi. When they had returned to the stables, and were handing the reins back to Johann, Rudi had invited her to ride with him the following morning, and any time, in fact, that she felt like joining him. Despite Mathilde's admonitions, she had no intention of passing up the pleasure either of riding, which she adored, or of doing so in Rudi's company, especially as he had suggested it. There was no harm in it, surely? He was merely doing his bit as a host, at a time of day when Gabi was still in bed. Gabi wouldn't mind, anyway — Kristal was sure of that.

* * *

At last the evening of the masked ball arrived. The house had been transformed during the preceding days. The large drawing-room had been restored to its original status as a ballroom, with banks of flowers everywhere. The dais where the grand piano usually stood alone was now ready for the musicians to set up their instruments. The wood-block floor had been lovingly waxed for dancing.

Along the corridors, discreet little notices had been affixed to indicate powder-rooms and cloakrooms, and to discourage guests from entering more private quarters.

After assuring themselves that all was in order, the two girls went up to don their nineteenth-century gowns. With daringly low necklines, Kristal's was a stunning lavender shade with a fitted bodice, an apology for sleeves draped over her upper arms, and a full, flaring skirt with tier upon tier of chiffon edged with lace. Gabi's was of turquoise silk, equally daring, with a fichu neckline and a flounced skirt gathered into clusters of palest pink rosebuds. She burst into Kristal's room as soon as she was ready. Kristal had just finished drying her hair.

"I suppose we ought to concoct nineteenth-century hairdos," she surmised aloud. "I'm not terribly au fait with them, though. Are you, Gabi?"

"Oh, don't worry about that right now. Let's go up and show Opa how we look. Poor darling, his arthritis is playing him up — he won't be able to come down at all tonight. I've got a wonderful idea, though. Come on, I want you both to hear about it together."

Kristal accompanied the younger girl to Gustav's room, wondering what she had in mind. They found him lying in bed, in considerable pain. It was much earlier than the time he usually retired.

"What do you think, Opa?" Gabi demanded, twirling in front of him.

"You look beautiful, darling. And

you, Kristal — give me a twirl."

She obeyed, with unconscious grace, gratified that their appearance gave her grandfather some pleasure when he was suffering so.

"I have a wonderful idea, Opa," Gabi declared.

She opened the bag she was carrying, and drew out two wigs, one dark, the other pale, each set in the style of the previous century.

"What a good idea, Gabi! That's going to save us a lot of bother. They look very natural, and," she said. "They're exactly the right colours, too."

"Excellent! Try it on!"

"That's the wrong one!" She laughed as Gabi thrust the dark wig at her.

Their grandfather began to laugh behind them. "Oh, I like it! With masks on, no-one will know which of you is which!"

Kristal looked uncertainly at the wig in her hands while Gabi eased the blonde one over her dark hair, already neatly pinned into a knot on top of her head. She then fixed on her jewelled mask, thereby hiding the part of her nose that differed from Kristal's. It was uncanny — looking at Gabi now was like looking into a mirror.

"Come back in the morning and tell me all about it," Gustav begged.

"You bet we will," Gabi assured him.

They both kissed him good-night and left him chuckling happily, helping him, perhaps, to forget his pain for a while.

They went back to Gabi's room, where she produced a bag of cosmetics and set to work, hiding the paleness of Kristal's skin. By the time she'd finished, no-one would guess they had swapped roles.

"Oh, you can't wear that," Gabi declared, as Kristal picked up her sapphire and diamond pendant, which was lying on Gabi's dressing-table. "I'm afraid you'll have to lend it to me. Do you mind? I mean is it very special?"

"Very! It belonged to my grandmother, but I've got a feeling she wouldn't have minded you wearing it."

"If you're sure. You're going to have to wear something of mine." She opened her jewel-case. "How about these?"

She lifted some stunning emeralds from their bed. They were set in gold, with matching earrings, and looked hideously expensive.

"Something simpler, I think."

They finally settled on a necklet of sapphires, which also had matching earrings. They looked heavier than her own delicate pendant, but were undoubtedly owned by Gabi.

"Will I do?" she asked Gabi.

"You'll do very well — Gabi," came Gabi's mischievous reply.

"Thank you, Kristal," was Kristal's giggled retort. "I'll just go and fetch my evening purse."

"I'll see you downstairs."

Back in her own room, Kristal picked up the purse and stared doubtfully in the mirror. It really was uncanny what a bit of make-up, a wig and a theatrical costume could do. Seeing herself like this, with glossy, dark hair, she almost felt like Gabi. But could she sound like her? She tried a tentative laugh, and then another, trying to mimic Gabi's tinkling sound. Then, she hurried from the room.

On the landing she saw Mathilde coming towards her from the other wing of the house. To her amazement there was actually some warmth in the smile on the old crone's face. She, too, was wearing an authentic, period gown, but in her preferred shade of grey. In her hand she held the mask she had not yet donned.

"Enjoy yourself, *liebchen*," she said. "And don't let the English witch steal your man from you."

Mathilde had been completely taken in by her assumed role! Kristal rather wished she hadn't, feeling cold inside on realising the extent of the woman's dislike for her. Nevertheless, she let out a quiet peal of laughter, sure that that would have been Gabi's response.

Going down into the hall below was like stepping into a time-warp. Everyone was wearing authentic clothes, the women in gorgeous gowns of every shade, while the men looked resplendent in the slightly starchier formal gear of the period. A few were even sporting false whiskers in authentic style.

They had done it, she thought, with a surge of triumph! They had laid on a nineteenth-century ball, and at the same time raised a large sum of money for charity. She set off towards the drawing-room, where the musicians were tuning up. Across the room she caught sight of herself in a mirror, then realised it was not herself at all — it was Gabi, chatting to Andreas. Surely she could not fool him? Yet by his attitude he seemed to be maintaining the distance he reserved for herself. There really was something in this body language business.

The musicians had finished tuning up. The conductor raised his baton and the first Strauss waltz began.

"Well, *liebchen*, I guess you and I are expected to lead off," Rudi said.

She looked up, surprised to find him not looking at her, but staring across at Andreas's blond head, now inclined towards Gabi's facsimile of herself, and very likely inviting her to partner him.

"Let's go, then," she said, and moved into his arms.

6

AT first Rudi's attention was fixed on the other couple but, after a few bars, he relaxed into the music, his hand, warm at Kristal's back, drawing her closer. "We dance so well together, Gabi, my love — just as we do everything else."

Kristal had to fight against the instinct to go rigid. What was he implying? "I'd like to dance with you alone all night, sweetheart, but people might guess our little secret. We'll have the supper dance and, after that — we'll play it by ear . . . ."

As the waltz ended, Kristal caught sight of the other couple leaving the floor on the other side of the room. Andreas, as he released Gabi, lifted her fingers to his lips, in an attitude of pure gallantry. Gabi turned to wave across to her, in a conspiratorial gesture, that indicated all was going well.

But was it? All the time she had been here, Kristal's hopes had swung from one extreme to the other, she now realised, on the one hand believing that Rudi was in love with Gabi, on the other hoping it was a more fraternal kind of love. His words tonight surely indicated it was very different from that.

Rudi had asked her to save the supper dance for him, so presumably she could dance with whoever she pleased until then. They had had to forego the tradition of dance-cards, since guests were supposed to be unrecognisable behind their masks. She was certainly not short of partners, though, and all of them, except Andreas, were complete strangers. Some of them wondered aloud whose face lay behind the mask, others openly called her Gabi.

It seemed, providing she steered clear of Rudi, the idea was fun after all. Except that she caught his elegantly-masked face turned in her direction on several occasions, and, from the tight set of his mouth, guessed that the eyes behind the mask held more than a touch of censure. It seemed he couldn't bear to see his Gabi in another man's arms. The pre-supper dance was at last announced and she could avoid him no longer.

"Are you having fun, my Gabi?" he asked huskily, drawing her into his arms.

"Of course," she replied, and, having downed a glass and a half of champagne, felt audacious enough to try a Gabi-type laugh. "It's brilliant!"

She felt him shake with laughter in that indulgent way he reserved for Gabi.

"We'll have even more fun later on, *liebchen*."

Kristal couldn't have answered if she had tried. She went hot all over at his words, as if a fever had entered her bloodstream. It was ridiculous, since she knew his words weren't meant for her.

The music stopped. It was time for supper, though she had suddenly lost her appetite. Rudi collected two platefuls of the tastiest morsels and proceeded to fork the food into her mouth, in the shady corner they found for themselves.

"Isn't it absolutely *prima*?" Gabi declared excitedly, when they met up later. "I'm not sure whether Andreas and Rudi have been taken in or not. They are both treating me exactly as I'm sure they usually treat you. How about you?"

"I suppose I could say the same thing."

"Rudi's being over-protective, I suppose."

"Something like that," she said warily.

"Come to my room and we'll touch up your make-up. How's Andreas acting with you?"

This time the question was rather more anxious. She could really get cross with Gabi, who appeared to enjoy having both men eating out of her hands.

"His usual charming self," she replied carefully, for Andreas, at least, had restrained himself to a few extravagant compliments.

In front of her dressing-table, Gabi removed her mask.

"I wonder if it was such a good idea. I've discovered something I'd really rather not have known. Mathilde's been horrible to you, hasn't she?"

"Hate at first sight, you might say," Kristal replied lightly.

"I'm truly sorry about that, Kristal. I can't understand why she should react in that way, but I got the full force of her venom just now. I do hope the rest of us make up for her rudeness." Gabi waited anxiously for Kristal's reply.

"Indeed you do," she replied. At least Gabi herself did, she thought silently.

No sooner had they returned downstairs than Rudi claimed Kristal in her Gabi look-alike wig.

"I think I shall keep you to myself for the rest of the evening," he murmured.

"That would hardly be circumspect."

"But look how we're delighting Mathilde!"

The old woman stood still and erect beside a pillar, a smirk — one could hardly call it a smile — of supreme satisfaction lifting her miserable features.

"Is that so important?"

"Let's put a real smile on her face," he whispered, and thereupon waltzed her out on to the terrace. There, he made no further pretence at dancing, instead gathering her fully into his arms.

"My own sweet love," he murmured huskily. "I can't wait till tonight. I want you so much. I want you now."

Her palms, in a hopeless attempt to restrain him, pressed defensively against his warm, solid chest. She could feel the play of muscle beneath her fingers, hear the rapid tattoo of his heart. His lips met hers then traced a line down her throat. She released a little whimper and clasped her hands around him.

"My God, you're beautiful," he whispered straightening up. "We will have to go back in, but soon all these people will be gone and I'll have you all to myself."

"Oh, Rudi," she murmured huskily, no longer playing a role.

"Later, sweetheart," he said and led her back into the ballroom.

The evening sped by far too quickly and, in no time at all, it was a few minutes to midnight, the appointed hour for unmasking. It was absolutely vital for Kristal to find Gabi. She espied her at the far end of the room and hurried over, seizing her arm to gain her attention.

"Hello. What is it, Gabi?" Gabi asked with a grin.

Kristal spoke softly, her words for Gabi alone. "Gabi, we must act quickly. It's nearly midnight."

"I know — I can hardly wait."

"We can't do this, Gabi — "

"Ssh — "

"We've got to swap — "

The orchestra stopped, and into the silence came the sound of the grandfather clock striking the hour. Amid much hilarity, people started to pull off their masks, revealing themselves, all except a laughing Gabi and a horror-stricken Kristal. Everyone stood around the two masked girls, waiting expectantly.

With a peal of laughter, Gabi removed her mask and then her wig, pulling out the pin holding her own top-knot and letting her glossy, black hair cascade over her shoulders. Andreas, now standing between them both, laughed.

"My suspicions have been confirmed," he declared. "I hope I was completely circumspect with you both."

"Completely," they agreed in unison.

There was nothing for it — Kristal reluctantly removed her mask and wig, to reveal the shimmering beauty of her own golden tresses. Guardedly, she sought Rudi's eyes. To her amazement and fury, he was shaking with laughter.

"You knew, didn't you?" she accused him in a stage whisper.

"I have to confess I realised at some point in the evening," he agreed.

"When?" she demanded now.

"Does it matter?"

"Of course it does!"

"I don't see why." He moved closer. "I hope your real persona won't refuse my invitation."

"Don't hold your breath!"

It was the last waltz and, to her chagrin, Rudi chose Gabi to dance with. As Andreas gallantly partnered Kristal she watched the other two with interest, unable to discern whether or not they were exchanging lovers' secrets.

The music ended. Rudi gave a little speech of thanks, announcing the staggering amount he estimated they had raised for charity that evening, and invited guests to make a final donation on their way out. Before the crowds dispersed, Kristal decided to make herself scarce. She had reached the stairs when she came face to face with Mathilde — a horror she had hoped to avoid.

"You think you've been very clever, don't you?" she spat without preamble.

"You mean you didn't enjoy our little joke?"

There was no way she was going to reveal it had been entirely Gabi's idea.

"It's obvious you enjoyed it very much! But you won't get him — I'll make sure of that. Even if you stoop to that kind of deception!"

"Deception?" Kristal queried with enforced coolness. "You mean you didn't realise before midnight? Rudi knew from the start."

She crossed her fingers behind her back, watching Mathilde's face turn even paler and then suffuse with anger. The older woman stormed off, leaving Kristal shaken by her malevolent expression. As a result, she slept badly that night, and, at a time when she would normally have risen, she fell into her most sound sleep of the night. Even Gabi had risen when she finally went down for breakfast.

"Are you all right?" the girl enquired, seeing Kristal's pale face.

"I'm fine, thank you. I always look dreadful when I oversleep."

"You should have got up and come riding — it's a wonderful morning."

The words came from Rudi who looked disgustingly fit, and Kristal wondered whether he had spent the night alone. Feeling Mathilde's rapier gaze she could not help remarking, "After a night like last night, I needed a lie-in."

A glance at Mathilde showed Kristal her remark had hit home. Mathilde had declared war and Kristal had decided to join battle.

"How about tomorrow?"

"Oh, yes, I'll be happy to go riding tomorrow."

Mathilde scraped her chair back and stomped out.

"What's got into her these days?" Rudi asked irritably. "She gets worse by the day." He drained his coffee-cup. "Anyway, I must get some work done — I'll be in my office if anyone needs me."

"Aren't you going to the bank today?" Gabi asked.

"No, *liebchen*, I'm working at home. Andreas is coming here later."

Kristal noticed the way Gabi's thick lashes fell, hiding their expression. The thought came to Kristal, once again, that this was indeed a house of secrets.

"I'll see you both later."

"I've been thinking, Kristal," Gabi began in an unusually serious voice. "Swapping roles with you made me very much aware of the difference in our lives. I'm just a useless, social butterfly, aren't I?"

"Oh, Gabi! What a ridiculous thing to say. I'd say you were an extremely useful social butterfly, if last night's anything to go on!"

"That's because you have a kind

heart! But seriously, I'd like to do something useful with my life, and I think I know what. I'd like to learn physiotherapy. I'm sure I could help Opa and people like him to lead fuller lives. I was reading about it. It's not good for arthritic people to sit about all the time. The more they keep their joints moving, the better it is for them. I don't mean Opa should get up on his bad days, but, well, if I persuaded Rudi to have a pool installed — "

"Is there room?"

"Masses of room. I don't mean a full-sized pool, but I'm sure part of the basement could easily be converted."

"What a splendid idea!"

"I'm going to find out about courses. I want to learn about hot wax treatments and massage — anything to help dear Opa."

"You're very fond of him, aren't you?"

"He's one of my favourite people. Speaking of which, we promised to tell him about last night. Come on."

Gustav was sitting in his usual, straight-backed chair, and in far less pain than on the previous night.

"I thought you'd never come!" he greeted them, an expectant gleam in his eyes. "Well, tell me all. Did you fool them? Did you have fun?"

"It was tremendous fun, Opa. Wasn't it, Kristal?"

"It certainly was," she agreed, holding her true opinions in reserve. "I don't know how many people we fooled, but most of them politely pretended we did."

"I think Andreas guessed early on."

Gustav's gaze rested on his dark-haired granddaughter, who mentioned Andreas's name with recurring frequency. "And Rudi?"

"I shouldn't think we fooled him for a moment — he's far too shrewd. Mathilde was pretty shocked when we unmasked and de-wigged, though."

"Shocked?" Gustav's eyes narrowed.

"From the things she said, believing me to be Kristal, she seems to have

126

misunderstood Kristal's reasons for coming here. At least, that was the impression I got."

"What did she say to you, while she thought you were Kristal?"

"Oh, I don't remember exactly," Gabi hedged warily. "But she made some reference to her grandmother, Analiese."

"What do you mean?" Gustav demanded.

"I don't think she liked her. Analiese worked in the library, didn't she?"

"That's right. She was a highly-educated, young lady. She came here to start the system of cataloguing we still use today, but she left quite suddenly, without even saying goodbye."

Both girls read more in the old man's sad eyes than either would admit. Kristal was becoming more and more sure that Mathilde had had a hand in Analiese's dismissal. Gabi changed the subject, and told Gustav of her plans.

"You want to do that for me?" he asked. Someone entered the room.

"Ah, Mathilde, has Gabi told you what she's going to do? She's going to become a physiotherapist, and help her arthritic, old Opa to become more mobile."

"That's utterly ridiculous! Rudi won't allow it. You're not some common working girl, Gabi. You're a von Steinberg, and von Steinberg girls don't go out to work. I can imagine who put that idea into your head!"

"I think it's an excellent idea," Gustav declared unequivocally. "And I think her motives are admirable, too. So don't go trying to discourage her."

"You've never spoken to me like that before, Gustav. You know I only have the best interests of this family at heart. I always have."

"The family's made up of individuals, each with a right to his or her own destiny. No-one should interfere with that whatever their motives."

His words had found their mark, and for once, Mathilde looked uncertain.

"I still think you should discuss this

with Rudi," she said stubbornly. "He has a right to some say in his future wife's life-style, surely."

"But it's what I want to do. If he doesn't approve, then I'm surely the wrong wife for him."

★ ★ ★

"I think I'll talk him round. Kristal, I feel I'm being kept in the dark about certain things, as if I need protecting from the harsher realities of life. I want to know the truth about Analiese, and why you really came to Vienna. Opa was in love with her, wasn't he?"

"Gabi, I don't think I should tell you. Rudi would be furious — "

"There you go again. For heaven's sake, I'm not a baby. If you have some skeleton in the cupboard, then I assure you I can take it. Or is it too terrible for you to talk about?"

"It would be a relief to talk about it, Gabi, but Rudi doesn't believe a word of my story, so I don't think I should burden you with it."

"Please tell me, Kristal. Surely I'm the best judge of whether or not I can take it. You can leave us here, Johann."

They had reached the centre of the city where Gabi led Kristal firmly into one of old Vienna's dark, wood-panelled coffee-houses.

"Well?" Gabi prompted gently once they'd been served.

"Oh, Gabi. I really shouldn't say anything."

"OK, let me make it easy. Opa was in love with Analiese — true?"

"True," Kristal agreed cagily.

"You and I are tall and slender. We have very different colouring. Our noses are different — but our eyes are the same, exactly like Gustav's mother. True?"

Kristal nodded, meeting eyes that mirrored her own. "True," she agreed.

"Is that a sheer fluke?"

Kristal shook her head.

"Then you don't have to tell me a

thing — except, why on earth they didn't marry. Gustav and Analiese, I mean."

"I really don't know all the facts," Kristal replied.

"Then I shall make it my business to unearth them," Gabi said determinedly.

7

HOWEVER displeased Mathilde might be, and however concerned Kristal felt about the old woman's veiled threats, when she awoke the following day to a perfect, summer morning, Kristal was determined not to miss her ride. Johann had taken to saddling up Gretel as well as Schwarzi, but as she had overslept the previous morning and therefore not ridden the saddled mare, it came as no surprise to Kristal to find Johann entering the kitchen when she went down.

"Mathilde asked me to check that you were riding this morning. 'It's not fair to Gretel to get her all excited and ready to go'," he mimicked the old woman.

Kristal laughed at his impression.

"Heavens, I didn't know she cared

132

about the horses — I've never seen her around the stables."

"She doesn't often come down, it's true, but I gather when she was young she was quite a horsewoman — so good, in fact, that she won dozens of prizes in the show-jumping ring. It's said she fell off one day, due to some careless stable hand, and never rode again."

Kristal absorbed these words with some surprise.

"Anyway, since you obviously are riding, I'll get Gretel saddled up."

With which he returned to the stables and she poured herself a cup of coffee.

"Waiting for me?" a deep, pleasant voice said behind her.

"No, actually, I'm finishing my coffee," she told Rudi, and explained what had happened.

"She's certainly unpredictable," he declared of Mathilde. "Come on, let's go. They'll be champing at the bit."

Johann was leading the horses around the stable-yard when they arrived. They collected their helmets, took over the mounts and were off.

As usual, they set off at a gentle trot, enjoying the early-morning breeze on their faces as they followed the bridle path to the woods. Once inside the woods, they contained the horses' energy as they headed for the long, straight ride some distance ahead. The path was wide enough at this point for them to travel side by side, and Kristal always enjoyed this part of the ride, when Rudi was disposed to talk to her without rancour, as if the very freshness of morning cleared away dark thoughts, giving way to a friendlier, more relaxed persona.

At last they reached the long, straight ride.

"I'll race you to the end." He laughed.

"You're on!" she shouted back, and gave Gretel her head.

At first she was in front but, before they had reached halfway, Schwarzi thundered past them. At the same moment, Kristal became aware that all was not well. Her saddle, unbelievably, was loose. She tried to rein in Gretel, but the mare was intent on catching up with Schwarzi.

Kristal screamed as the entire harness slipped and she lost the battle to stay on. Her cry brought Rudi up short. He looked back, and then turned his horse and galloped back to where she lay, leaving Gretel, who was now slowing down, to her own devices. For an instant, he towered above her figure lying motionless on the ground, then leaped down beside her.

"Kristal!" he breathed hoarsely. "Speak to me, *liebchen*. Kristal!"

The breath had been knocked out of her body and she ached all over. She forced heavy eyelids open.

"Rudi," she murmured, squeezing her eyes shut as tears welled up.

"Are you all right, sweetheart? Where does it hurt?"

"Everywhere," she replied.

"I'll kill him!" he seethed under his breath.

With amazing gentleness, he ran his hands over her limbs, establishing that nothing was, in fact, broken.

"We're not far from the lodge," he told her. "If you can't bear the thought of getting on Schwarzi in front of me, I can go and fetch a car from there, only I don't really want to leave you here alone."

He lifted her to a sitting position, holding her in his arms.

"I'll get on Schwarzi," she decided, nestling into his cradling arms and resting her aching head on his broad, reassuring chest.

The sound of other hooves shattered the silence of the woods, and a rider came into view. A very flustered Johann slid down from his horse. Rudi gently but swiftly released her, then snatched up his riding crop and struck his erstwhile friend a blow across the shoulders, shouting with an anger Kristal would not have thought possible.

"For goodness' sake, let me tell you what happened!" Johann yelled. "You don't think I'd let a horse leave the stables like that, do you?"

"What do you mean?" Rudi demanded.

"It was that old witch, Mathilde. She came to the stables this morning. It's the first time in years. She pretended to be concerned about Gretel being saddled up yesterday, and not getting a ride. Anyway, she sent me to the house to make sure Kristal was going to ride her. That's when she must have done it."

"Done what?" Rudi demanded hoarsely.

"After you had gone, I found a pair of shears in the hay where Gretel had been tethered. They're always hanging securely in their proper place on the wall. Only Mathilde had been there since I oiled and replaced the tools last night. It was only a suspicion, but I came after you, to make sure you were all right, hoping I was wrong."

"The bloody woman's gone mad!"

Rudi's attention returned to Kristal, while Johann went over and retrieved the mare's harness. Tears were running freely down Kristal's face now. How could anyone hate her so much?

"Don't cry, *liebchen*," he begged.

"As I feared," Johann said. "See, it's been cut almost right through. The rest would have torn with the stress of the gallop."

"As Mathilde must have intended. Look, I'll stay here with Kristal while you fetch the car from the lodge, Johann. Tell Meggi to prepare the room next to mine. I'm sorry about — " He gestured towards his discarded riding-crop.

"Forget it. I'd have done the same. I think we shall both need the doctor," he joked to Kristal, rubbing his shoulder.

When they arrived at the lodge after a comparatively smooth ride, but one which reminded her of every little bruise, Rudi carried Kristal up the stairs, while Meggi fussed around like a mother hen.

"The bed's all made up and I've switched on the blanket. She'll be cold, poor mite. Dr Seigal will be here soon."

Kristal found herself laid gently on a large four-poster of dark, carved wood. It matched the other heavy pieces of furniture. The room was lightened however, by pale walls and carpet, and by the palest pink curtains hanging at the windows and round the bed, matching the plump, feather-filled duvet.

"This was my mother's room," he told her.

"It's lovely," she told him wearily, unable to keep her eyes open.

"I think you should try to stay awake, my love," he advised her. "At least till Dr Seigal arrives."

He left to allow Meggi to help Kristal out of her clothes, but then returned to stay with her, berating himself for not taking greater care of her.

"Something will have to be done about Mathilde," he said absently.

"She really hates me," she mumbled, tears flowing anew.

"Don't," he begged, taking her fully into his arms, letting her cry into his tweed-covered shoulder.

He was still holding her when Dr Seigal walked in. The doctor was about Rudi's age, with clever, grey eyes behind rimless glasses.

"Ah, you got here at last, Wolfgang," Rudi said jokingly.

"I'll come by rocket next time. Wait outside, Rudi, and send Meggi in."

He examined Kristal minutely for any sign of injury. Nothing, she thought, could escape his careful scrutiny.

"You're a lucky girl," he told her at last. "You'll ache all over for several days. You have extensive bruising. You could have suffered a lot worse. Stay in bed till you feel like getting up. I'll leave some tablets for the pain. Thank you, Meggi. You can let him in now — he'll be champing at the bit."

"Well?" Rudi demanded impatiently, when Meggi opened the door.

Dr Seigal repeated what he had told Kristal.

"Rest is what the girl needs, together with some of Meggi's excellent home cooking. She'll be right as rain in no time. Look after her."

"I intend to," Rudi replied huskily.

It was Rudi who brought her up a light lunch of home-made soup, cheese and fruit.

"Johann has gone back for your clothes. Gabi can pack what you need."

"I'm sorry to be such a burden," she apologised, knowing he was a busy man, with little time to spare for anything but work.

"I hardly think you should be apologising. I'm surprised you're not screaming for a lawyer!"

"I wouldn't do that."

He was looking at her strangely. "No, I didn't really think you would."

That afternoon, Kristal fell into a deep, restorative sleep. Several times she drifted upwards through layers of slumber, aware of a solid, comforting presence and lean, but gentle, hands that stroked her brow and the line of her cheek, of a deep voice murmuring words to soothe her troubled mind.

She woke to find his arms about her.

"Can I get you anything?" he enquired.

"A cup of tea would be wonderful. And a painkiller? I've got a dreadful headache."

"Of course. Meggi's gone to her sister's," he told her then. "Her sister's just come out of hospital. She didn't want to go, but I assured her I was quite capable of looking after you. If you had been badly injured, Wolfgang would have whisked you off to hospital right away, as I told her."

"B-but what about your work? You ought to be at the bank now, surely?"

"It means Andreas and others will just have to work a bit harder, that's all. He'll have less time for more personal pursuits that sometimes tempt him from the office," he told her drily.

"Did Johann bring my things?"

"He did. Gabi wanted to come along, but Wolfgang insisted you were to be kept quiet — I don't think Gabi's brand of gaiety fits in with his prescription."

"It was kind of her, though."

"She doesn't know exactly what happened," he told her carefully. "Merely that you fell off a horse."

"A-and Mathilde?"

"I'll deal with her in my own good time. No-one has been told how badly, or otherwise, you've been injured."

The tea Rudi brought was deliciously refreshing, though she couldn't touch the pastries Meggi had made.

"I'd love a bath right now," she thought, as he removed her cup, not realising she had spoken the words aloud.

"I'll run one," he replied, and promptly disappeared through the door to the adjacent bathroom.

She listened to hot water gushing into the bath, and smelled the fragrant steam that wafted back to her, from the oils he must have added. The water stopped running and Rudi reappeared. "Can you manage?" he asked.

"Yes, thank you," she assured him quickly.

"I'll leave you now," he told her, "but don't try to be heroic — if you can't manage, I'll be right back. I'll even close my eyes, if you like."

She returned his smile gratefully and, when he had gone, slipped off her remaining clothes, crept slowly into the bathroom and lowered herself gingerly into the vast, porcelain bath, not feeling at all brave, but determined to manage.

The warm water soothed away some of her aches, but it was difficult to get comfortable. Some of the worst bruises were where she sat down and she moved gingerly from side to side, trying to find a position that didn't hurt. After soaping herself, she decided to be really ambitious and wash her mud-caked hair, managing the task quite well.

She got out of the bath and wrapped

a voluminous towel round herself. She walked slowly back into the bedroom and pulled on a pale-blue, satin nightdress. Then she called Rudi.

He was there almost immediately.

"All done?" he asked.

"Yes," she replied and hobbled painfully to the bed and climbed in.

"I brought some books up while you were in the bath," he said. "I'll go down and start supper while you see if there's anything there that takes your fancy."

The choice of reading surprised her. There were some modern German novels and a book of poetry; there were several recent bestsellers by English and American authors. There was also a book on Austrian history, with as many illustrations as there was reading matter. On further investigation, it proved to be a history textbook for children.

She looked for the author's name: R. W. G. von Steinberg, in other words, Rodolfo Wolfgang Gustav von

Steinberg. It was written by Rudi himself.

Although it was in German it was still quite easy to read, since it was written in simple, straightforward language intended for children. She had soon laid aside the other books, as the history book caught her attention.

History had never been like this at school, she thought, as she read on, almost annoyed when Rudi interrupted, appearing with a nourishing, casseroled stew and an apricot flan, that looked absolutely delicious.

"I can't allow you to eat alone," he told her. "I brought mine up, too, to ensure you don't just pick at your food."

"I won't do that, anyway," she assured him. "I'm starving! I've been waiting approximately three hundred years for this meal!"

He shot her a glance that suggested she had gone crazy, then noticed the book in her hand. He laughed.

"I see! Are you interested in history?"

"I would have been if our history books had been this interesting!"

"I'm flattered. I think history should always be presented in an interesting way to children. Otherwise they're lost from the start. Put it down now and take this tray. You must eat everything on it, as I prepared it myself — all except the flan."

"Jawohl; Herr Ober!" she joked. He really was a man of surprises and, as she looked across at him, his handsome features highlighted by the soft glow of lamps, she thought she had never loved him more.

8

THE following day, Kristal woke from her after-lunch nap feeling pleasantly refreshed.

"How are you?" a familiar, deep voice asked, startling her.

"Ouch!" she groaned. "I thought I was feeling better till I moved!"

"Would you like to come downstairs for a while?"

"Oh, yes, please," she accepted at once, her face lighting up at the idea. "I need a wash first, though."

"Right, then. You have your wash and then we'll see how you feel about it. Don't try to come down alone, though," he warned.

The effort of washing and dressing made her weak with fatigue, but she was determined to demonstrate her independence so, clad in sweatshirt and jeans, she started to descend the stairs. She had managed three stairs, clutching the bannisters tightly, before Rudi found her.

"What did I say?" he demanded crossly, lifting her into his arms.

"I thought I could manage," she muttered.

At the foot of the stairs he paused and looked down into her intensely-blue eyes. Her lashes drifted over them, in case she revealed the depth of her feelings for him, but not before she had observed a strange look akin to tenderness in the amber depths of his.

"Down you go, then," he said softly and lowered her slowly to the ground. Her arms were reluctant to leave his neck, but as they slid down his broad chest his own arms encircled her body, drawing her firmly against him.

"Think you can walk now?" he asked.

"Let go of me and I'll try."

"I'm not sure I want to do that."

To her consternation, his head

lowered and his firm, sensual lips found hers.

The brief touch sent a shivering ecstasy through her body. She wanted to kiss him back, to prolong the kiss indefinitely, but he was already releasing her, his arms sliding away. Her legs felt weak, whether from that kiss or from being in bed she didn't know but, as if understanding, he placed a supporting arm about her waist and helped her into his cosy sitting-room.

"Down!" he yelled to the dogs, who had bounded forward to greet her.

With backward glances of disgust and disappointment they returned to their bed in a corner of the room. Rudi settled Kristal in a vast, comfortable armchair near the hearth where huge logs were sending out a blissful warmth. "Will you be all right in here?" he asked doubtfully. "I'll fetch your book, or you can listen to music, if you prefer."

"Perhaps a little Mozart?" she said,

smiling shyly. "And I would like my book. Where are you going to be?"

"Er, I thought I'd do a little work in my den."

"For the bank?" she enquired, harbouring a suspicion it was not.

"No, actually, on my latest book."

"If it turns out as interesting as the one I'm reading, you'll have a best-seller on your hands!"

"I hardly think so. Text-books don't feature in such lists, more's the pity."

"Couldn't I sit and read in your den?" she asked tentatively, reluctant to be alone, while he worked in another room.

He seemed to consider the idea. Maybe his den was a private retreat, where no-one else was allowed. Perhaps she shouldn't have asked.

"Why not?" He shrugged. "You're a restful enough person to have around."

She glowed at the compliment, suddenly absurdly happy. Her smile lit her eyes to sapphires and arrested his progress across the room. He stood there, his own eyes lit by the smile on his lips.

"You're beautiful when you smile — you should do it more often," he told her.

"There hasn't been a lot to smile about recently," she replied.

"No, I agree, and I'm sorry about that. I must do something about it."

He walked out of the room, but soon returned with the book. Lifting her gently to her feet, he helped her across the room, and into his den.

She had imagined something smaller. This was no tiny hideaway. This was obviously where Rudi did what he would consider his real work. Solid bookshelves, ranged round two sides of the room, were filled with arduous-looking tomes, and files stacked in neat piles. Doubtless Rudi knew where to find anything he needed, though probably no-one else would.

On a large, mahogany table stood a practical, modern lamp, angled over some documents which he must have been working on, together with several books and files. In a corner of the room, an L-shaped table was groaning under the weight of office equipment: an up-to-date colour computer, phones, a Telex, and, that indispensable piece of hardware — a facsimile machine.

"Heavens, what a hive of industry! I think I ought to make myself scarce."

"Nonsense! I told you you're restful to have around."

She hadn't wanted to leave, anyway. There was an armchair near the fire and it was there that he directed her. Halfway across the room she caught sight of the wall opposite the window. Most of its surface was taken up by some kind of chart, like a vastly intricate map. She paused.

"That looks interesting. What is it?"

"A dynastic chart."

"May I see?"

She walked slowly across to it. Rudi flicked a switch and a picture light came on, lighting up the wall with its complicated chart.

"How fascinating! The Hapsburg dynasty!"

"Plus descendants and antecedents. This red line indicates the line of rulers."

"And this blue line?"

"Oh, that's just the von Steinbergs," he told her dismissively.

"You're related to the Hapsburgs?"

"Distantly," he shrugged.

Just before he switched off the light she caught sight of another name: von Rosenburg. That had been her grandmother, Analiese's family name. She would take a closer look some time. Right now, the last thing she wanted to do was upset Rudi, and spoil the delightful truce they were enjoying. She allowed herself to be installed in the chair by the fire and started to read, only occasionally glancing up to where Rudi was working.

She tried not to appear too curious when the phone rang. It was clear from his enthusiasm, though, that someone had unearthed something important.

"It sounds like another piece of the jigsaw," he said into the phone. "Could you send it through?"

A few minutes later the facsimile machine started to disgorge the vital information. In the end, Kristal gave up trying to read and sat gazing into the fire.

"I think I'm the one distracting you," Rudi said and laughed lightly.

"Not at all, but I couldn't help overhearing your conversation. It all sounds fascinating."

"It is," he agreed, tearing the page from the machine and perusing it carefully. He selected an old, leather-bound volume from a bookshelf.

"Would you mind checking this reference for me?" he asked, laying the book on a table beside her, together with the Fax he had just received.

"You mean I can help?" she cried, turning pink with pleasure.

"I thought you might like to justify your existence," he replied drily. "You might look in these, too."

He added a couple more books and soon she was busy turning pages, checking indexes and making notes.

After that, it became a regular thing. Kristal suspected he was humouring her, or trying to prevent her getting bored.

It was some time before she plucked up the courage to mention the chart again. She probably would not have done so at all, but one morning he returned with some coffee to find her studying the chart.

"What's so interesting?" he enquired.

"Oh, nothing, really."

He put down the tray of coffee.

"So which 'nothing' line was holding your attention?" His eyes picked out the line her finger had located. "Does von Rosenberg mean something to you?"

"It was my grandmother's name before her marriage," she admitted huskily.

"And do these names mean anything to you?" he asked, suddenly alert.

The line ended with a Heinrich von

Rosenberg, born in 1861.

"Heinrich was the name of Analiese's grandfather," she said quietly.

"Is that so? Well, I may just follow up this line then. Perhaps there's a relationship there. If this Heinrich was Analiese's grandfather, then you're more closely linked to the Hapsburgs than the von Steinbergs!"

Dr Seigal looked in every day, his visits becoming more social than professional, for, after a few days, Kristal's bruises had ceased to hurt very much, and she was able to walk unaided.

She had been there for over a week. Meggi had still not returned, and she was wondering when Rudi would suggest that she, herself, leave for the house in Vienna. She didn't want to bring this little idyll to an end by suggesting it.

"Do you feel up to a walk in the woods?" Rudi enquired that evening.

"I'd love it!"

In the west, when they started out,

the sun was just a faint light above the trees, suffusing the sky with splashes of brilliant coral. Alone she might have found the atmosphere sad, but with Rudi it was tranquil and companionable.

There was nothing tranquil about the two labradors, however. Kristal joined in their game and they suddenly realised they were on to a good thing, with two people to play with them. Raben bounced back, a stick in his mouth, and tried to leap up to return it to her.

"Down, Raben!" Rudi roared. "This girl is fragile."

Duly chastened, Raben took off through the undergrowth with Honig.

"I don't think I've ever been called fragile before," Kristal said with a grin. "People usually regard me as big and capable. It's nice to be thought fragile."

Rudi was so big, so strong, he made her feel very feminine, almost dainty.

"You wouldn't be laughing at me,

by any chance, would you?"

"No! I told you — I like it," she insisted.

He stopped and turned towards her. The look in his eyes had her heart turning somersaults. He moved slowly, as if in a dream, his arms reaching for her, drawing her against his hard body.

"You're more beautiful than any porcelain," he said huskily. "Warm and real, inside and out. Do you know what it's done to me, having you here in my home, with no-one else around, knowing I must keep my hands off you?"

"Rudi," she murmured protestingly.

He murmured her name in return and then his lips were on hers.

How long the kiss lasted Kristal had no idea, nor did she want it to end, but by the time he raised his head, the first evening star had pierced the sky. She lifted wide, dazed eyes to his, grateful for the hands supporting her.

159

"Let me love you, *meine liebchen*," he begged softly.

The sound of a car shattered the moment, and stopped her confessing her love. The low, satisfying growl of an expensive sports car gradually came closer.

"That sounds like Andreas!" Rudi released her so quickly she almost fell. "Of all the times to turn up! Come on, we'd better get back."

Not only had Andreas come, he had also brought Gabi who, when they reached the house in the wake of the dogs, hurled herself into Rudi's arms.

"Rudi, darling!" She kissed him in the vicinity of his mouth and then turned to embrace Kristal. "How are you, Kristal? Has he been looking after you?"

She looked stunning as usual. Kristal felt decidedly underdressed in her sweatshirt and jeans. She also felt distinctly left out when Gabi and Rudi, with easy familiarity, put their arms about each other and went ahead into the house, leaving herself and Andreas to follow.

"I suppose you both want to stay for dinner?" Rudi enquired drily.

"We came to take you out!" Gabi said enthusiastically.

"I don't think so," Rudi declined. "Kristal's had a bad time. I don't think she's up to gallivanting just yet."

"In that case, we'll stay," Gabi declared. "I'm missing you both so much! Opa's a bit under the weather, and Mathilde goes about with a face like a sour lemon. I would have been so bored, if it weren't for Andreas. He's been keeping me amused."

"Not in office hours, I trust," Rudi commented sternly, and turned to Andreas. "All is well at the bank, I hope?"

"Nothing untoward has occurred since I spoke to you this morning."

"Well, don't let Gabi distract you — not if you want that seat on the board."

"As if I would!" Gabi cooed

dismissively. "But poor Andreas! All work and no play and all that — while you two have been cloistered away here in the middle of nowhere, without even Meggi as chaperone!"

"That's enough!" Andreas snapped, and the others turned to look at him with varying degrees of surprise. "You do go over the top sometimes, Gabi. Can't you see you're embarrassing your cousin?"

"Oh! Oh, Kristal, I'm sorry. I was only joking, I swear."

"It's all right," Kristal told her. "If you'll excuse me, I'll go up and change."

"May I come up with you? I have so much to tell you," Gabi said excitedly.

"Of course," Kristal replied, leading the way to her room. "So, what have you been up to?" she asked as she started to undress.

"I've arranged to take private tuition in physiotherapy. I'm going to work part-time in St Josef's Hospital while I study for the qualifications. I've already started, in fact," she ended triumphantly.

"So you haven't exactly been bored out of your mind?"

"Did I give that impression?" she enquired with a grin. "I just haven't told Rudi, in case he didn't approve. Andreas doesn't think I should go ahead without telling him — Andreas has a few doubts about it."

"I'm not sure Rudi would object. Anyway, what do you do at the hospital?"

"I'm only doing voluntary work — you know, changing library books, bits of shopping, arranging flowers, serving drinks — that sort of thing." Gabi's expression turned serious. "Do you really think Rudi wouldn't object?"

9

RUDI and Andreas were in the kitchen when the girls returned. Andreas had chopped ingredients for a salad, and was busy mixing an interesting-looking dressing. Rudi was preparing steaks. Two bottles of claret sat on the table, one of them already open.

Rudi's gaze swept briefly over Kristal. "Very nice," he approved with a little nod. "Help yourselves to wine. Oh, and could you lay the table, Gabi?"

"We both will. I'm not an invalid. Come on, Gabi."

"I think you've done enough for one day," Rudi warned.

She, on the other hand, preferred to keep busy, to avoid thinking of that heavenly walk in the woods, and that kiss and how it had felt to be in his arms.

164

The superb food and wine restored everyone's good humour, for they had all seemed a trifle edgy earlier. A Linzertorte which Gabi found in the vast freezer rounded off the meal.

"What shall we do now?" Gabi asked brightly.

"What do you want to do?" Rudi enquired indulgently. "I suppose it's too much to hope you'd be content just relaxing and listening to music?"

Kristal would have loved to do just that, especially if they had been alone.

"We could play charades," Gabi suggested.

"I think we had enough of that little game at the masked ball!" Rudi said.

"Let's play poker, then."

And for the next hour or so they played a very informal game of poker, using matches for stakes.

"I'm surprised Rudi hasn't disappeared into his den," Gabi remarked at one point. "He usually does when we're here. It's his inner sanctum — no-one else is allowed in there."

Kristal shot a startled glance at Rudi, for they had spent hours in there together. The glance he returned was quite unfathomable. Was it true, she wondered. Was she the only person privileged to enter his private world?

The hall clock struck midnight.

"I think we'd better call it a day," Gabi declared, yawning widely.

"Just because you're losing!" Rudi said, laughing at her indignant expression.

"I'm tired," she said, looking as lively as ever, but stretching languorously.

"I'd better take you home," Andreas said quietly.

Gabi met his glance and for seconds their eyes were locked.

"Would you mind awfully if I stayed here tonight?" she asked timorously.

She had certainly put him on the spot, and for an instant he looked livid.

"I would, actually, but since you appear to have decided what you want, I must accept your decision."

There seemed to be an underlying

message in his words, and it was clear to Kristal what it was: both men were in love with Gabi, and she had just made it plain that her preference was for Rudi.

"I suggest you see Andreas out," Rudi said, gathering up the cards. "You can pay us the millions you owe us another time."

"Or win it back!" She laughed.

Kristal gathered up their glasses and took them to the kitchen. She was just plumping up cushions while Rudi set the fire-guard in place when Gabi returned.

"I think I'll go up," she said, not looking at either of them. "The usual room, Rudi?"

"Yes," he agreed.

"I think I'll go up, too," Kristal said.

"You must be tired. Good-night, Kristal." His lips brushed her cheek.

As she lay in bed, restless and uncomfortable, realising she had done too much and stayed up too late, she wondered which 'the usual room' was. Was it Rudi's? Was that why Andreas had looked so furious?

By morning, after a night of little sleep, Kristal's mind was made up. She had stayed too long already in this family. She had met and got to know her grandfather, and already felt a strong affection for him — despite his supposed treatment of Analiese all those years ago. She had also made a friend of fun-loving Gabi. In that respect, her visit had been a success. She had come looking for relations and she had found some.

On the other hand, she had come to realise she could never be part of their family; for she had unwisely allowed herself to fall in love with Rudi, who belonged to Gabi. Hence, she had decided to return to home, and to do so without telling Rudi.

It was still early; there was no sound of life as yet within the ancient walls. After showering, Kristal dressed and packed the remainder of her clothes.

When she opened her door to go down for breakfast, she thanked heaven for her decision, for Rudi and Gabi were walking towards her, their arms nonchalantly around each other's waists.

Kristal fought down a spear of jealousy as she addressed them.

"Good-morning, you two," she said brightly.

There was a slight scowl of puzzlement marring Rudi's handsome brow, but Gabi rushed forward, linking arms with her.

"Good-morning to you, Kristal. How are you this morning? I was just saying to Rudi how good it would be if you were to return to Vienna with me. I've missed you so much. I — "

"That's exactly what I've decided to do." She carefully avoided Rudi's eyes. "Rudi's been so good to me, but I'm feeling heaps better, and quite ready to face the world again."

Rudi was unusually taciturn over breakfast, though Gabi chattered on, unrepressed. After the meal she went up to collect her things for the journey, leaving Kristal alone with Rudi.

"I don't think you should go yet," he told Kristal bluntly.

"Why not?"

"You'll recover faster here," he replied. "Besides, I want you to stay."

"Why can't you be content with one woman?"

"One?" His hand moved to cover hers where it lay on the table. "I want you, Kristal. I want you here, with me."

She stared at his handsome face, his dilated eyes and, despite the knowledge that he was utterly despicable, calmly telling her he wanted her when he had just spent the night with Gabi, her heart began to race, a heat building up inside her, numbing her mind and eroding her resolve.

"Well, that's everything," Gabi trilled happily.

Her voice preceded her into the

room, giving them time to move apart.

"Mathilde will have gone by the time we get home," Gabi declared.

"Gone?" Kristal enquired in astonishment, looking to Rudi for confirmation.

"I've decided a month in Baden will do her good," he affirmed. "She'll be catching the train right now. If you're determined to go, Kristal, I'll drive you both back — it's time I put in an appearance at the bank, anyway . . . "

After depositing them at the von Steinberg residence, Rudi only stayed long enough to don a business suit before setting off for the bank. He looked in on them where they were having coffee.

"I'll see you this evening," he told them both. "Auf Wiedersehen."

"Wiedersehen," Gabi murmured. Kristal muttered a choked, "Goodbye."

"I'm going back to England," she told Gabi baldly, once the sound of his car had died away.

"You can't! When?"

171

"Today — I'm feeling a bit homesick," she lied.

"But you have no-one in England!"

"I have a job, and friends," Kristal reminded her gently.

"I can't bear it." To Kristal's chagrin, tears welled up in Gabi's eyes. "You can't go! You're the sister I've always wanted. Please don't go — not yet."

"I must," she replied quietly. "If I don't go soon I shall no longer have a job to go back to, and my friends will have forgotten me. But I must go up and see Gustav before I go."

Gustav was standing by the window, looking frail and hunched and leaning heavily on his walking-stick, when Kristal went in to see him.

"Good-morning, Gustav. It's good to see you out of your chair," she said.

His face was shadowed, but she could see the serious expression in his eyes, when he said, "Come and sit down, Kristal."

"I've actually come to say goodbye, Gustav."

"I'm not surprised. Rudi told me about the wicked thing Mathilde did — how she caused your accident."

"He did?"

"I'm not a child to be cosseted, the way he cossets Gabi. She doesn't know, of course. Not yet, anyway. Will you tell me about Analiese before you go? Did she really run away to the arms of a new love, as she told Mathilde?"

"Is that what Mathilde told you?"

He nodded, his eyes never leaving her face, desperate for the truth.

"No, she didn't."

"Seeing you, I can no longer believe that story. Mathilde must have traced her to England — maybe she wrote from there. If Mathilde also discovered that my Analiese married someone else, it would only add fuel to her story. You are my granddaughter, aren't you, Kristal? You have to be — you have my mother's eyes, just like Gabi, though Analiese's golden hair."

Hearing his wavering voice brought

a lump to Kristal's throat.

"Yes," she admitted quietly. "I am your granddaughter. My grandmother was very badly treated. When the housekeeper learned that Analiese was pregnant, she apparently told a member of the family. I realise now that that member must have been Mathilde. She told my grandmother that you wanted her to leave. You were away in Paris, on business."

"I remember. I also remember how devastated I was to return and find my love gone — to the arms of another lover, according to my scheming sister."

"She did no such thing — she made for England where she met David Hastings. He knew about her pregnancy, but he still wanted to marry her. She liked him well enough, and fell in with his wishes."

"Were they happy together, Analiese, this David Hastings and my son?"

"I'm afraid the war, fate, call it what you will, denied them that chance. Only hours after the wedding, David was recalled to his unit. He was killed shortly afterwards. They were never truly man and wife. You were Analiese's only love."

"My Analiese. Forgive me, my Analiese," he begged of her departed spirit.

"Of course she would have forgiven you. You were being manipulated just the same as she was. I doubt she would have forgiven Mathilde, though."

"I doubt that I can, either. It was a wicked, wicked thing she did."

"I suppose she had your interests at heart. Were you happy with Elfrieda?"

"Happy? No, I wouldn't say we were happy. She was Mathilde's best friend, and Mathilde had always pushed her in my direction, hoping we would marry. She was always jealous of Analiese."

"But not of Elfrieda?"

"No. I was not in love with her, and they had always been friends. She was not my choice of wife, but since I could not have Analiese, I settled for her. The two women ran the house, and I pursued my own interests."

"How cruel fate has been."

"Perhaps. If you have the good fortune to love and be loved, let no man, or woman, get in the way of it."

His words were heavy with meaning, yet they had no relevance to herself. She was indeed in love, but the object of her love actually loved, and was going to marry, someone else.

"I'm glad we've had this talk before I leave," she told him. "And that the truth is out at last."

"So am I." His gaze fell on her sapphire pendant. "She kept it, then?"

"You mean it was a gift from you?"

"Indeed."

"It was always special to her, just as it is now special to me."

"I'm glad. Don't stay away too long, will you, *liebchen*? We've all grown inordinately fond of you, with the obvious exception, of course."

He meant Mathilde, of course. Little did he know that Rudi's fondness was limited to a physical desire for her.

"I won't," she assured him, wishing she could mean it. She stood up and kissed his wrinkled brow. "*Auf Wiedersehen*, Opa."

10

HER first few weeks back in England, in what promised to be the coldest summer in years, were the most wretched Kristal could remember. Her thoughts frequently strayed to the clear, balmy days she had enjoyed in Austria.

There was plenty to keep her occupied. For a start, there was Analiese's home in Dorset to be sold. Before she could put it in the hands of an estate agent, she had to go through all her grandmother's possessions. This proved a harrowing task, reminding her as it did of the happy times they had spent together over the years.

Kristal eventually sorted everything out, keeping a few favourite items which she arranged to have transported to her flat in London, and putting everything else in the hands of auctioneers.

When she returned to work, Jeremy and Sheila Robards, who owned Robards' Fashions, were so delighted to see Kristal walk in on her first day back that they stood up in unison and cheered.

"Thank goodness you're back, darling," Jeremy cried dramatically. "Your department's been a disaster without you."

"I don't believe you."

"Seriously," Sheila assured her. "The temp's caused chaos. Oh, dear, Kristal, I've just noticed — you look absolutely terrible."

She explained away her pallor by blaming it on the accident, not mentioning the man who filled her mind and heart by day and stalked her dreams by night.

Work was something of an antidote to her misery, at least by day, but there was no respite by night. When, one morning, a letter bearing an Austrian stamp landed on her doormat, she pounced on it, disappointment hitting her as she recognised Gabi's rounded scrawl.

After a paragraph or so of delightful but unremarkable trivia, Gabi went on:

We're all missing you so much! Opa keeps asking when we're going to persuade you to come back. He misses your chess games. He seems to have lost his liking for practical jokes, too. I think without Mathilde around to frown and disapprove, there's no incentive. She apparently took to Baden, and has decided to rent an apartment there.

Without you to curb my extravagances, I've reverted to the shopaholic syndrome, I fear, though I have less time for shopping these days. I'm working very hard at my studies, and I really enjoy my regular stint at the hospital, especially helping in the children's ward. I want to have lots of children.

I met Andreas on one of my shopping trips, Gabi went on. *He said Rudi's just as grumpy at the bank as he is at home.*

He goes about like a bear with a sore head these days.

You really should have said goodbye to him, Kristal, after he took care of you so well. I think he's quite hurt by the way you took off without a word to him.

We had planned to take you on a boat trip to Budapest. You would love it. Since you weren't here, we went alone, and on the way back he formally proposed, and I accepted. Oh, Kristal, I'm so happy, now that it's decided.

Kristal, on the other hand, felt as though a dagger had been plunged into her heart.

We're getting married in mid-September. You will come, won't you, Kristal? As I have said before, you are the nearest thing I have to a sister, my dear English cousin, and, naturally, I want you to be my bridesmaid. I'll have your dress made — to fit me. We're exactly the same size, remember? It was such fun at the masked ball, but I also learned what it was not to be me . . .

Kristal could read no more through the haze of tears. Gabi and Rudi were to be married and Gabi wanted her to be bridesmaid. How could she bear it, watching the two of them taking their vows? She couldn't do it. Yet, if she declined, Gabi would be hurt and insulted, and Rudi might guess the truth.

It took over a week to pluck up the courage to reply, but, at last, she picked up a pen and did so.

Congratulations to you and Rudi on your coming marriage, and of course I'll be delighted to be your bridesmaid. I'm afraid I can't take any more time off work until then, so it's a good thing we wear the same size. I look forward to seeing you all, she ended, which was partly true.

A few more letters were exchanged, always between herself and Gabi. Well, she could hardly expect Rudi to write himself, could she? As his future wife, it was natural that Gabi should organise things.

For Kristal, the summer passed in a daze. The mantle of rainy, grey sky barely lifted, farmers prayed for some late sunshine to ripen their crops, and summer slid slowly into an unrelenting autumn.

She arrived in Vienna the day before the wedding. Johann picked her up and drove her to the house under a soft blue, Austrian sky. Elegant buildings along the route glowed benignly in the gentle sunlight. This was where she belonged, she felt it in her heart, yet it was where she could never be.

When she entered the house, full of apprehension, dreading her first sight of Rudi, Gabi rushed forward to embrace her.

"Thank you so much for coming, Kristal. I can't tell you how happy I am to see you." She hesitated. "Rudi's not here — we shan't see him till tomorrow."

"How is he?" she said, trying to hide her relief.

"He's fine."

Which told her nothing at all.

"And how's O — your Opa?"

"And yours! He's told me, at last. Now that I'm to be a married woman, everyone's starting to treat me like an adult! You and I really are cousins, and quite close ones, too . . . "

She babbled on happily, and Kristal wondered if Rudi, also, knew and accepted the truth.

"How are you getting on with the physiotherapy?"

"Fine! I'm really enjoying it. Fortunately, my husband-to-be is quite happy for me to carry on, you know, indulge the little woman — except that it really is important to me to be doing something useful. He'll soon realise that. Of course, when the children come along . . . " Suddenly Gabi grabbed her by the arm. "Come on, Opa's dying to see you!" she cried.

Gustav stood up as they entered his room. His movements, she fancied, were a fraction smoother than she remembered.

"I told you we'd get you back here somehow." He chuckled. "How do you think I look? Young Gabi here has been putting me through my paces, bullying me into walking a little every day. Swimming, too."

"Swimming? You mean you have the pool she was planning?"

"We have, indeed. She's quite relentless! Little minx — I'm sure someone else would be only too happy to give the baggage away!"

"You're giving her away at the wedding? Oh, but that's wonderful!"

"Why do you think I've been bullying him?" Gabi laughed happily.

"And Mathilde won't be there to sour the occasion," Gustav informed her, to Kristal's relief. "She's staying on in Baden."

"I can't pretend I'm sorry."

"No," he agreed gravely. After a pause, he declared, "It's almost time for my swim, but I shall join you for dinner."

Sure enough he did, but, though he

185

and Gabi proved entertaining hosts, there was an essential ingredient missing for Kristal. Rudi was not there, and would never be there for her. When the others decided on an early night, she was glad to turn in, feeling strangely tired and deflated.

The wedding day dawned. The two girls dressed together, with the help of the dress designer, and a hairdresser who arranged their hair. Gabi looked a vision in a bridal gown of stark white silk overlaid with Bruges lace. It had simple lines, with long, fitted sleeves, a sweetheart neckline and a skirt that extended to form a train. A small, diamond tiara held in place her long, lace veil.

"You look wonderful, Gabi," Kristal told her. "An absolute vision."

"So do you!" Gabi laughed.

The dress she had chosen for Kristal was of exactly the same design, but of blue silk beneath the lace, and minus the train.

"It's a beautiful design, Gabi."

"We could do a swap when you get married!" The sparkle dimmed in Kristal's eyes, but she forced a smile to her lips. "It's a pity you've lost weight, but the sash takes up the slack. Now I'm fatter than you!"

Perhaps Gabi had an inkling of how very nervous she felt at the prospect of witnessing their marriage. She wouldn't even ask how Andreas was taking it.

"You and I are travelling in the same car with Opa — I've an idea I shall need help with him. He'll stay in his chair till the last moment, but he's determined to walk up the aisle and give me away, whatever he says to the contrary."

A large crowd was waiting at the church to see the bride. There were gasps of delight and exclamations of surprise as not one, but two, tall, beautiful girls emerged from the car. Johann had driven them there and now helped Gustav to get out with as much dignity as possible. He had agreed to use his wheel-chair as far as the church

187

door, but there, he stood up slowly, and proudly offered Gabi his arm. As Kristal moved into place behind them, Gabi turned to give her a ravishing smile that expressed her own delight, and somehow gave Kristal the courage she needed for the ordeal ahead.

She inhaled deeply as they crossed the vestibule and entered the main body of the church. Gabi moved forward slowly on Gustav's arm, though who was supporting whom it was difficult to tell. Kristal followed a few paces behind. She kept her eyes at the level of Gabi's waist, aware of two tall men in shadow at the top of the aisle, both turned to watch their progress to the altar. She was quite unable to lift her eyes and face the inevitable a moment sooner than she had to.

Guests on either side looked on the dark-haired bride with admiring eyes, while many an appreciative glance went to the fair bridesmaid behind. Organ music swelled to fill the vaulted splendour of the church, gradually silencing till there was only a vibrating echo as they reached the waiting priest.

Kristal still kept her eyes forwards as someone assisted Gustav to a seat and Gabi turned to hand her bouquet to Kristal. A tall, grey-suited man moved to stand beside Gabi, looking down at her with all the tenderness of a loving bridegroom.

Kristal's head swam with a strange confusion, for it was Andreas who stood beside Gabi, not Rudi. Rudi was there, right beside him, in the best man's position. The colour drained from her face and rushed back. She thought for a moment she would faint.

"Are you all right, *liebchen*?" Rudi asked at once, taking a pace backwards.

One strong hand grasped her elbow, lending the support, both physical and mental, that she desperately needed right then.

She looked into amber eyes that held a hint of concern.

"Kristal?" came Gabi's worried query,

while Andreas merely shook his head, disassociating himself from Gabi's final prank before she became his wife.

"I'm fine," she assured them both, as the priest cleared his throat, waiting to begin the service.

There was the whole of the service to get through, hymns, prayers, the blessing, the signing of the register, all of which gave Kristal time to come to terms with the fact that Gabi was marrying Andreas, not Rudi. What was more, she was the only person who hadn't known. If she had been a guest, and received a formal invitation, Kristal, too, would have known.

So how was Kristal supposed to react? With surprise, presumably. And that's what she would do. She would go along with it, but she would also make her escape at the first possible moment, she decided, as she followed the newly-weds back along the aisle, this time on Rudi's arm.

The contact was almost unbearable. Glancing up, she met eyes that scorched her to her very soul. It was no good, she told herself furiously. Not once had he attempted to get in touch, yet the message in his eyes was clear.

"Were you surprised?" Gabi wanted to know, while photographers chivvied them this way and that.

"Of course I was! I distinctly remember writing to congratulate you and Rudi on your coming marriage in one of my letters."

"That's when I got the idea! I realise my own letter to you must have caused the confusion."

"You write as you talk, my love," Andreas said. "In a torrent of confusion."

"How can you say such a thing?" Gabi laughed.

"Because it's true!" Rudi put in.

The newly-weds were ushered into their car, while Rudi led Kristal to the Mercedes. Johann was sitting behind the wheel. This was the biggest ordeal so far, being alone with Rudi.

"You really thought I was marrying Gabi?" he asked as the car pulled away.

"Naturally — that was what she allowed me to think."

"And how did you feel about that?"

"Feel? What should I feel? It was what I expected, of course. Since Mathilde took great pains to point out your unofficial engagement almost the moment I arrived, it came as no surprise."

"If you had known Gabi was marrying Andreas, would you still have come?"

There was a tension underlying the words. Kristal pondered a moment. What did he want her to say?

"Of course," she replied with enforced coolness. "Gabi wanted me as her bridesmaid. Whom she was marrying made no difference."

Her fingers were clasped so tightly about her flowers that the knuckles showed white. He reached over and covered them with one large, warm hand.

"I'm glad you came." His thumb traced circles over her sensitive wrist. "You and I have some unfinished business to attend to."

"I don't think so," she denied, now thoroughly alarmed. He was virtually declaring his intentions, and they had always been strictly dishonourable.

Some of the guests had arrived at the house before them, and now formed elegant, little groups as they meandered across the drive.

"Have you kissed the bridesmaid yet?" somebody called to Rudi. "It's the best man's privilege, don't forget."

"So it is," he agreed with a grin, and turned her into his arms.

"Rudi, no," she begged.

She couldn't bear it, Rudi kissing her, and in front of all these people. His arms slid to her shoulders as his head lowered, their bodies just touching but, as their lips met, they swayed together as if that was where they belonged. His lips slid over hers, with a gentle, undemanding pressure that made her long for more. She couldn't stop the little moan of satisfaction that rose in her throat, any more than she could prevent her eyelids closing as her lips responded to his.

At last, without deepening the kiss, he raised his head.

"You wouldn't get away so lightly if we were alone," he informed her.

She couldn't answer for emotion. She still loved him and wanted him as much as ever, and it seemed he still wanted her — but that was all. A couple more hours and she would definitely make her escape.

Ignoring the ribald comments around them, Rudi grasped her arm firmly and led her indoors to form part of the reception line-up. Gustav was there with them, in his chair once more, and enjoying himself immensely.

"I'm glad you're having one of your good days," Kristal told him warmly, when all the guests had arrived.

"I don't have so many bad ones now," he replied. "My little Gabi is doing wonders for her Opa. I'm only sorry I don't have both my granddaughters in Vienna. Would you perhaps consider making your home here with us, *liebchen*?"

"I — I don't think I could do that," she told him regretfully, for all the while she had been in London, Vienna had lived on in her heart. "My work — "

"Of course." He patted her hand. "I understand. It's going to be strange, having Andreas living here instead of Rudi."

"Rudi doesn't live here any more?" she repeated stupidly.

"You didn't know? No, *liebchen*. Andreas has been elected president of the bank. Rudi resigned — it was never his cup of tea. He'll stay on the board — he's too good a banker to lose entirely. No, he now lives full-time at the lodge, closeted in that den of his, most of the time. Andreas is a much more dedicated banker, and, since this is Gabi's home, it makes sense for him to move in here. It's all worked out rather well — except for you, Kristal.

Think about it — we'd all love to have you here."

"Thank you, Opa," she replied.

Kristal just had to escape. The laughter and gaiety of the Austrian crowd served to pinpoint her misery. Turning down a nearly-deserted corridor, she heard the voices of children ahead. The morning-room had been cleared and set aside as a creche, where guests' children could play games and be looked after by a pair of hired children's nurses.

"Do come in," one of the nurses called, as Kristal hovered by the safety gate fixed across the doorway. "It's easy enough to open from that side."

"Which one is yours?" the second nurse enquired.

"None," she confessed. "I just felt like escaping for a while, and was attracted by the noise."

"You must like children — most of the guests are trying to avoid us!"

One small boy stood apart from the rest, clutching a toy elephant, too

196

young to join in the rougher activities.

"Don't you want to draw a picture?" Kristal asked, kneeling beside him.

He shook his head.

"Would you like me to tell you a story?"

He nodded.

"My name's Kristal. Will you tell me yours?"

"Manfred," he pronounced carefully.

"Is that what your mother calls you?"

"She calls me Fredi," he admitted. "Can I call you Fredi?" He nodded. "Shall I tell you the story of Thumbelina?"

As she embarked on the story, some of the other children clustered round her. She abbreviated the story to a realistic length and was just about to end when she became aware of a dark shadow in the doorway . . .

11

AS Kristal looked up to meet Rudi's scorching gaze, he strode with ease over safety-gate barrier and came towards her.

"And they lived happily ever after," he finished for her. "And now I'm about to whisk away your story-teller. She's wanted elsewhere," he explained.

"Wiedersehen, Fredi," she said, and allowed Rudi to open the gate for her. "Who wants me?" she enquired curiously.

"I do," he replied, taking her arm and leading her into the study.

"I really should get back. I've been absent for ages."

"A little longer won't hurt, then," he replied determinedly and pulled her into his arms. "Will you come to the lodge with me when the reception is over?"

"No, I most certainly won't!" She struggled to escape, but his arms became steel bands around her. "Now, let me go — I have to get back."

"Not till I've persuaded you," he replied, cupping her face in his hands. His lips sought hers, brushing teasingly back and forth. One hand cradled her head, the other wrapped round her slender waist. She pressed her palms to his chest, and felt the pounding of his heart.

"Say you'll come," he said, at last ending the kiss.

"I — I can't," she replied, already faltering as she knew she would.

He sighed, as if in defeat. "We'd better get back," he said.

They had reached the middle of the hall when she heard Gabi call to her.

"Come and help me change!" And Kristal hurried after her.

Glancing down as she sped up the stairs, she met Rudi's bemused gaze, and once more felt the power of those scorching, melting eyes. Why did she have to love him so? Love was such a complicated and complicating emotion.

"You weren't just surprised to discover who the bridegroom was, were you?" Gabi asked tentatively, as Kristal helped her out of the bridal gown.

"Astonished," Kristal insisted, trying not to sound as flat as she felt.

"I — I saw your face, Kristal. I'm so sorry. You weren't even just astonished, were you? You were deeply shocked, and I think I know why. You're in love with Rudi, aren't you?"

"Yes," she agreed simply. "I'm afraid so."

"Oh, Kristal! I'd never have played such a cruel joke, had I known."

She disappeared into her shower, leaving Kristal to mull over what had happened. Rudi had made it perfectly clear that his only interest in her was physical, and that was all there was to it, which was why she had to take herself out of his orbit just as quickly as was decently possible.

"What do you think of my going-away outfit?" Gabi enquired as she re-emerged, wrapped in a large, fluffy towel. She waved a hand at a lavender, cashmere suit and toning blouse, which were hanging on a wardrobe door.

"Absolutely gorgeous!"

"I had a shopping spree only last week. I bought you something, too. Here."

She produced a large box bearing the name of a well-known fashion house. On opening it, Kristal withdrew a suit of very similar lines to Gabi's, but in a cinnamon shade, and a cream, silk shirt.

"I've already had my present! Oh, they're beautiful, but I couldn't accept them, Gabi."

"Well, of course you could. What would I do with them? They're your colours. They wouldn't suit me."

"All right — to please you. Can I use your shower first?"

Kristal disappeared into the bathroom and re-emerged a few moments later wearing the new outfit.

"What did I tell you!" Gabi exclaimed. "They're perfect on you."

"You don't look so bad yourself! Why didn't you marry Rudi?" she found herself asking.

Gabi laughed, a delicious peal of joy.

"I couldn't marry Rudi! Oh, I adore him, of course, but he's always been like a big brother to me."

"You mean, there's never been any romance between you?"

"Good heavens, no. Mathilde had this ridiculous hope about Rudi and me. We humoured her, but we never went along with the idea ourselves. I'm sorry."

"I'm sorry, too, that I misunderstood. I just couldn't see how Rudi wouldn't be in love with you. You're a much more effervescent person than I am."

"Which drives Rudi mad at times! Anyway, you've had little to be effervescent about, losing all your family, being alone in the world, and then coming here, to find yourself facing downright hostility from at least one member of the family."

"At least one! You mean Mathilde, of course?"

"Yes, I do. But I realise now that Rudi wasn't exactly welcoming, at first. He changed his tune when you were hurt, though. He really was upset when you ran out on him without a proper goodbye."

"Well, I'm sorry about that, but I'm afraid I'm about to do the same thing. There's only one thing Rudi's interested in, as far as I'm concerned, and I love him too much to settle for an affair."

Gabi did not reply and Kristal turned to find out why — Gabi was never short of words. She was holding a lipstick to her mouth but not applying it.

"Do you think this is a good colour to go with this outfit? Or is it a bit too purple?" she asked, changing the subject abruptly.

"I think a slightly paler one would be better. Try this one," Kristal suggested, picking up one that was pinker, but still slightly lilac.

"There! Will I do?"

"You look wonderful!" Kristal enthused. Her expression turned serious then as she asked, "Would you do me one last favour?"

"Anything! I'm so very happy you came — even though you believed I was marrying the man you love! I only hope you find the happiness Andreas and I share. So, what is it?"

"Have a discreet word with Johann, and have him bring the car round to the side entrance in half an hour. There's a flight I want to be on."

The brilliance in Gabi's eyes dulled. "If that's what you really want."

After apologising to Gustav for the brevity of her stay, Kristal collected her things. She used the back stairs, praying that Johann had got her message and would be waiting. Sure enough, the black car with its tinted windows was right there, the engine ticking over quietly. The boot was open so she lifted her case in and climbed in through the open back door.

Ten minutes later, she began to feel puzzled. This was definitely not the road to the airport. She tapped on the glass partition to speak to the peak-capped driver. He removed the cap and their eyes met in the mirror.

It was Rudi, she realised with shock, not Johann, at the wheel, and his amber eyes were glittering with fury. Furious herself, she slid back the partition.

"I don't know what you're playing at, Rudi, but I want to get to the airport immediately, and this is not the way!"

Without a word he drove on, heading for the Wienerwald, and not stopping till they had reached his house, right in the heart of it. The car came to a halt, with a screech of rubber on gravel. Flinging open his door he climbed out, wrenched the back door open and pulled her from the car.

"What are you doing?" she asked tremulously.

"Did you really think I'd let you run away from me again?" he rasped harshly.

Any further protest she might have made was cut off by his mouth on hers. She resisted, remained rigid for as long as she was able, but the battle was lost from the start. With a stifled sob, she threw her arms round his neck and held him close.

"See," he murmured huskily. "You belong with me. Come, *liebchen*. You and I have to talk."

He unlocked the door. There was no-one to let them in — Meggi was still at the reception. Once inside, he guided her to his den. He switched on the lights and while he lit the fire laid in the hearth, she went over to the dynastic chart.

"You've added more lines," she commented.

"That's right, I have." He came to stand beside her. "Here, in the centre, you have the Hapsburgs. Over there, the von Steinbergs, and on the other side, slightly closer to the royal house, you have the Rosenbergs: your great-great-grandfather, great-grandfather, and," he said and pointed with a ruler, "your grandmother, Analiese, then your father, Andrew von Rosenberg/Hastings, and finally, yourself, *liebchen*."

"You've added our names!"

Tears sprang up behind her eyes. She looked again, dashing away the tears. Beside Analiese's name she saw (=*Gustav von Steinberg*).

"They weren't actually married," she said unsteadily.

"In their hearts they were. I've had a long talk with Gustav, and also with Mathilde. Were it not for her, they would have married, and you would have grown up here, in Vienna, where you belong — and where I hope you'll decide to stay."

"I've already told Opa I can't," she explained, "and I wouldn't want to get under Gabi's and Andreas's feet, when they've just got married."

"You wouldn't need to. I want you here with me, in my home."

"Wouldn't Meggi be shocked?"

"Shocked? She's been telling me for years it's time I married some nice, little fraulein, and raised lots of little von Steinbergs." He drew her into his arms.

"Will you marry me, Kristal?" he asked with unaccustomed humility. "I know I don't deserve you, but I do love you. I even hoped — "

"I love you, too," she assured him, removing the troubled uncertainty from his brow. "And yes, I'd love to marry you."

"My love," he said, his eyes scorching into her soul. Then their lips met in a long, searing kiss . . .

WITH SOMEBODY ELSE
Theresa Charles

Rosamond sets off for Cornwall with Hugo to meet his family, blissfully unaware of the shocks in store for her.

A SUMMER FOR STRANGERS
Claire Hamilton

Because she had lost her job, her flat and she had no money, Tabitha agreed to pose as Adam's future wife although she believed the scheme to be deceitful and cruel.

VILLA OF SINGING WATER
Angela Petron

The disquieting incidents that occurred at the Vatican and the Colosseum did not trouble Jan at first, but then they became increasingly unpleasant and alarming.

DOCTOR NAPIER'S NURSE
Pauline Ash

When cousins Midge and Derry are entered as probationer nurses on the same day but at different hospitals they agree to exchange identities.

A GIRL LIKE JULIE
Louise Ellis

Caroline absolutely adored Hugh Barrington, but then Julie Crane came into their lives. Julie was the kind of girl who attracts men without even trying.

COUNTRY DOCTOR
Paula Lindsay

When Evan Richmond bought a practice in a remote country village he did not realise that a casual encounter would lead to the loss of his heart.

ENCORE
Helga Moray

Craig and Janet realise that their true happiness lies with each other, but it is only under traumatic circumstances that they can be reunited.

NICOLETTE
Ivy Preston

When Grant Alston came back into her life, Nicolette was faced with a dilemma. Should she follow the path of duty or the path of love?

THE GOLDEN PUMA
Margaret Way

Catherine's time was spent looking after her father's Queensland farm. But what life was there without David, who wasn't interested in her?

HOSPITAL BY THE LAKE
Anne Durham

Nurse Marguerite Ingleby was always ready to become personally involved with her patients, to the despair of Brian Field, the Senior Surgical Registrar, who loved her.

VALLEY OF CONFLICT
David Farrell

Isolated in a hostel in the French Alps, Ann Russell sees her fiancé being seduced by a young girl. Then comes the avalanche that imperils their lives.

NURSE'S CHOICE
Peggy Gaddis

A proposal of marriage from the incredibly handsome and wealthy Reagan was enough to upset any girl — and Brooke Martin was no exception.

A DANGEROUS MAN
Anne Goring

Photographer Polly Burton was on safari in Mombasa when she met enigmatic Leon Hammond. But unpredictability was the name of the game where Leon was concerned.

PRECIOUS INHERITANCE
Joan Moules

Karen's new life working for an authoress took her from Sussex to a foreign airstrip and a kidnapping; to a real life adventure as gripping as any in the books she typed.

VISION OF LOVE
Grace Richmond

When Kathy takes over the rundown country kennels she finds Alec Stinton, a local vet, very helpful. But their friendship arouses bitter jealousy and a tragedy seems inevitable.

CRUSADING NURSE
Jane Converse

It was handsome Dr. Corbett who opened Nurse Susan Leighton's eyes and who set her off on a lonely crusade against some powerful enemies and a shattering struggle against the man she loved.

WILD ENCHANTMENT
Christina Green

Rowan's agreeable new boss had a dream of creating a famous perfume using her precious Silverstar, but Rowan's plans were very different.

DESERT ROMANCE
Irene Ord

Sally agrees to take her sister Pam's place as La Chartreuse the dancer, but she finds out there is more to it than dyeing her hair red and looking like her sister.

HEART OF ICE
Marie Sidney

How was January to know that not only would the warmth of the Swiss people thaw out her frozen heart, but that she too would play her part in helping someone to live again?

LUCKY IN LOVE
Margaret Wood

Companion-secretary to wealthy gambler Laura Duxford, who lived in Monaco, seemed to Melanie a fabulous job. Especially as Melanie had already lost her heart to Laura's son, Julian.

NURSE TO PRINCESS JASMINE
Lilian Woodward

Nick's surgeon brother, Tom, performs an operation on an Arabian princess, and she invites Tom, Nick and his fiancé to Omander, where a web of deceit and intrigue closes about them.

THE WAYWARD HEART
Eileen Barry

Disaster-prone Katherine's nickname was "Kate Calamity", but her boss went too far with an outrageous proposal, which because of her latest disaster, she could not refuse.

FOUR WEEKS IN WINTER
Jane Donnelly

Tessa wasn't looking forward to meeting Paul Mellor again — she had made a fool of herself over him once before. But was Orme Jared's solution to her problem likely to be the right one?

SURGERY BY THE SEA
Sheila Douglas

Medical student Meg hadn't really wanted to go and work with a G.P. on the Welsh coast although the job had its compensations. But Owen Roberts was certainly not one of them!

HEAVEN IS HIGH
Anne Hampson

The new heir to the Manor of Marbeck had been found. But it was rather unfortunate that when he arrived unexpectedly he found an uninvited guest, complete with stetson and high boots.

LOVE WILL COME
Sarah Devon

June Baker's boss was not really her idea of her ideal man, but when she went from third typist to boss's secretary overnight she began to change her mind.

ESCAPE TO ROMANCE
Kay Winchester

Oliver and Jean first met on Swale Island. They were both trying to begin their lives afresh, but neither had bargained for complications from the past.

DoM

▓ **Hounslow** Leisure Services

Library at Home Service
Community Services
Hounslow Library, CentreSpace
24 Treaty Centre, High Street
Hounslow TW3 1ES

Working in partnership with ▓ Hounslow

0	1	2	3	4	5	6	7	8	9
670	361	3082)	3970	565	906	30 557	6538	419	
	751	972	373	874		260 (2)	3049	306A	
			903	704	9525	826 2087	208		6689
			973	644		346	3087	818	639
			7583			206		808	
						926		268	
						146		408	
						7226	1588		
						116	3087	2087	
						6496	9587		
							9507		

P10-L-2061